THE CUP AND THE PRINCE

KINGDOM OF CURSES AND SHADOWS I

DAY LEITAO

sparkly wave

Cover illustration by Natalia Sorokina (J Witless)

Print ISBN: 978-1-9992427-7-0

Please note that this is an advanced reader copy and that it will differ slightly from the final book. Adjustments might include typesetting, fixing typos, and cover adjustments.

Thank you so much for reviewing this book! Reviews are important and your work is appreciated.

THE CUP AND THE PRINCE

To everyone who dreams about a world without walls.

1

CREATURES FROM THE SHADOWS

Zora had always wanted to be a hero. Honorable, selfless, brave. She used to think that with enough hope and belief, everything was possible.

Tonight, she'd had enough of it.

Contrary to what stories told, being petty, revengeful, and deceitful felt amazing. If she were to risk a bet, she'd say it felt even better than what she'd been about to do. Not her. Some silly past self. Goody-goody-hopeful-nice-girl Zora. Let them think so. Some might say she'd snapped. Nope. She had awoken. And seen the light.

Not literal light. It had always surrounded her. Names are deceiving. The Dark Valley was likely the most well-lit place in the kingdom. Perhaps even in the world. Torches, bonfires, and lamps everywhere, all the time, just in case there was a pesky cloud from who knows where. Of course, sometimes the wind broke a lamp's encasing. Sometimes someone forgot to add oil to a lamp. Other times, a bucket was left upside down, or a piece of clothing was carelessly thrown somewhere. It happened. Perhaps it was unavoidable. And that brought pain, fear, and death to her valley.

Despite everything, there was also hope. She saw it in the eyes of every laughing child. It was hope that kept her going, hope that prevented her heart from growing cold. Except tonight. Tonight, she was fueled by anger. And it was so much more powerful than hope.

But this story is getting messy, so we'll get back to the beginning.

Four hundred years before...

Too early?

Let's go back four hours then, when Zora was still bright-eyed and oblivious.

THIS WAS NOT LIKE in stories or in the way Zora had expected. It should be natural, romantic. It should evolve effortlessly, the natural expression of a couple's love. Instead, she sat on the edge of the bed, stiff as a tree. Seth had no shirt on, the light from the setting sun coming through the transparent curtain and giving his well-defined abs a golden hue. He looked good, as always, staring at her from his dark brown eyes, through his golden, sunburned hair. Zora herself had hair just below her shoulders, dark brown in the roots, with golden tips. Her eyes were hazel. Everyone said they were a beautiful couple. A couple. And the idea tonight was to couple. She thought so but didn't feel it.

They would be kissing had the situation been different. She wouldn't be looking at him as if he were a human shadow ready to pounce on her. Well, he wanted to pounce on her. And the idea had sounded wonderful. She'd been thinking about it the entire day. But now that they were there, alone, somehow it was all different.

Seth sat by her and ran his hand through her hair. "Hey, relax."

His smile put her at ease. A little. She had a nervous laugh. "I'm trying."

"I'll help you."

He brushed his lips on her, and then they were kissing. It was Seth. Seth, the guy she loved. The guy she'd kissed—and often more than kissed—for the last five months. More than that, he was the valley's hero, their hope. This was his goodbye gift.

For the first time, someone from the Dark Valley would be allowed to compete in the Royal Games. Seth, having grown up fighting dark creatures from an early age, would obviously squash his competition. He would be their voice to the king and return in glory. He would show them what the Dark Valley people were made of. For now, all he was asking was for Zora to inspire him and make sure he wouldn't forget her.

These were all very nice and valid reasons for them to be there. Nice and logical. And now that he was kissing her shoulder and lowering her straps, for some reason the logical outcome seemed horrific for her. Seventeen. Zora was seventeen and shouldn't be acting like that.

She put a hand on his chest to get some distance. "Can't we wait?"

He puffed and rolled his eyes. "Zora. We've had this conversation."

She got up. "You're leaving tomorrow. I'm not saying no. But when you come back. We'll have more time. We could just... do the usual."

Seth took her hand and kissed it. "Am I not your hero?"

Zora sighed. "Yes."

He got up, towering over her, his hand now on her shoulder, playing with her strap. "Don't you want me to think about you every time I win a challenge? Don't you want to share a piece of my victory?"

Yes. And no. Zora's mind was whirling. Would he forget her if she said no today?

He didn't wait for her to answer. "And you promised."

She looked down. "I did."

It wasn't just Seth that she was letting down, but herself, too. This was not how she'd imagined this would happen, and she hated to be acting like a scared fifteen-year-old. She fought shadow creatures from time to time, and now she was terrified of *this*? Ridiculous. Perhaps she could just lie down, close her eyes, and tough it out. For Seth. But the thought made her sick in the stomach. As much as her mind wanted to convince her that this was right, her heart—and body—weren't there yet.

This had been her choice, her decision. But now she wanted to decide something else and was getting confused. And scared. More like terrified.

And then none of that mattered, as screams came from outside.

In seconds, Zora was outside and running, her sword Butterfly in hand, heart tight thinking she knew who these voices belonged to: some of her students. And that meant it was children who were being attacked. And it couldn't be. As much as she tried to teach them how to defend themselves, they weren't ready. They weren't ready. And there had been no warning. No gongs had been rung.

And then she saw it. A shadow wolf running towards the central square where there was indeed a group of children. Zora swung her sword, hit the shadow creature, but didn't manage to kill it. It kept running towards the kids, but she couldn't catch it. In the middle of the square, boys and girls had their swords drawn. Little Layla ran forward. No, no. The girl was barely eleven. Too young. Too young to die or be mauled for life.

Zora couldn't even breathe. Time stretched and she could hear her heart while trying to run after the creature. Then she heard something behind her and turned. A human shadow was almost on her. With two fast strokes, Zora killed it, and the creature disappeared, leaving just some smoke behind. Seth had just killed another shadow wolf. Then there were no more creatures, but Layla was fallen, blood on her forehead and hair.

Zora ran to her. "Hold on."

"She killed it," one of the kids said.

And might have been killed in the process. The girl had a gash on her face. People were coming from out of their houses, some of them looking horrified. Seth was beside Zora, kneeling. "I'll carry her to your house."

Little Layla had fear in the eye that was still not covered in blood. Before Seth lifted the girl, Zora looked at her and smiled. A calm smile, telling her that her wound wasn't that bad, that it would all be all right. A smile of hope. Some of the fear left the girl's face.

Seth carried the girl to Zora's house, or rather, her parent's house.

They were preparing a bed and getting potions ready. Her mother caught a breath when she saw Layla's wound, but then quickly gave the girl a sleep draught.

Her father was quick to start cleaning and stitching, ignoring the girl's screams of pain. Zora held little Layla's hand, still keeping what she thought was an encouraging smile, a calm mask of fake tranquility. Layla didn't need to know how bad her wound looked. She had to hope.

There were voices far away; her mother preventing the girl's mother from entering, Seth saying he would come back later, someone outside. Layla fell asleep, stitched from her cheek to her forehead. The gash had missed the eye. One thing to be thankful for.

Like all the kids Zora taught, Layla spent most of the time learning combat and self-defense techniques. Tonight it might have saved her life. Zora wished she could teach them more, more about medicine, more stories, more things to make sure they could still dream. She did it when they were practicing training routines. Sometimes she wondered if it was right to try to encourage these kids to hope. Would they ever leave their valley? Generation after generation, they were paying for something someone might have done hundreds of years before.

When she was younger, Zora believed they were the defenders of the kingdom, keeping the darkness from spreading. Only later would she learn that the valley was basically a prison, a punishment for dealing with dark magic, keeping in generation after generation the descendents of the people who had allowed those creatures to spawn. Sometimes she still told herself her old lie, tricking her mind that they were there because they wanted to. But then, there was Seth. Seth was leaving. Seth was perhaps bringing help. Change was possible.

Zora went outside after Layla fell asleep. There were people talking, discussing. They wanted to know how those creatures had come to the heart of the village. Rangers were sent to look for dark spots. It was always like that; when a shadow creature spawned, they pointed fingers at each other or at least tried to find where they'd messed up. Perhaps it was their own way of hoping. Hoping that one day they'd figure it all out and no longer make any mistakes. Was it possible to avoid mistakes?

There were four types of creatures: humans, which had a human shape, but with grey skin. They were common, not much faster or stronger than a person, but they had claws sharp as knives. Then there were the wolves, four-legged creatures, not really wolves, as they didn't have a particular shape. They were fast and dangerous, strong, and had sharp claws and teeth. There were also spiders. When it was just a small space, like a bucket upside down, they spawned. About the size of an apple, they had sharp pincers and deadly poison. At least they didn't spawn on trees, bushes, or anything natural, but they could show up under a carelessly thrown piece of clothing, for example.

But the worst creatures were the balls. They were round and could be small like a spider or big like a human, and they exploded. At least they were rare. They were called shadow creatures because they spawned in the shadows, but names are deceiving. They were solid and real as if they were living beings. The main difference was that they disappeared instead of dying and didn't bleed. But killing them was like killing a real person or animal; by hitting it with a sword or something sharp. People in the valley, including Zora, usually enchanted their swords to make them stronger, sharper, and more deadly against the creatures, so that they disappeared with fewer blows.

The best way to fight shadow creatures was to prevent them from ever spawning, making sure everything was always well-lit. And yet somehow they could never manage it. There was always an accident. Always someone hurt or killed. And that was why everyone had to know how to fight. Zora had faced wolves, humans, spiders, and even balls. It was part of life in the Dark Valley.

Would it ever change? Zora walked aimlessly. She wanted to curl up and cry, but if she broke down, what would her students do? Her students' ages varied from seven to twelve, big enough to learn to defend themselves and yet too young to be helping to light up the mountain or the forest. She tried to encourage them, inspire them, tell them that everything was possible. And yet, there they were; the heart of their village still vulnerable.

Zora needed some time alone, some time when she wasn't trying to pretend to be brave or calm or hopeful. She leaned on the outer wall of a house in the village and took a deep breath. Even though she was alone and troubled, her ears were perked. In the silence, it wasn't hard to notice when a shadow creature was coming, and that could be the difference between life and death. But all she heard was the wind. Then more wind, and then the wind bringing the sound of a voice.

"It won't be the same without you." That was Razi, Seth's friend. He had a low, obnoxious, raspy voice she would recognize anywhere.

"You'll get used to it." That was Seth. Another voice she would never mistake, but his was smooth. "I'm not gonna say I'm sorry for leaving this prison."

Razi laughed. "I won't say I'm not jealous. It might sound silly, but I would give anything to see the girls in court. I've heard that even the maids there are hotter than the girls here."

Typical Razi, always thinking about girls, bragging about girls.

Seth laughed. "Being hotter than the girls here doesn't mean much."

What did he mean by that? Maybe he was just playing

along with his friend. Still, Zora couldn't help the nauseous feeling growing in her stomach.

Razi laughed, then asked, "What about your girl? How is she taking it?"

Zora perked up.

"Taking what?" Seth sounded almost annoyed.

"You leaving her?"

Leaving her. Well, yes. Unless he meant... not coming back? But Seth was coming back.

"I haven't said anything. If she wants to cry for me, cry when I'm gone." His tone... was mocking? Or was she mishearing it?

"Why?" Razi had a teasing laugh. "You haven't made her cry with joy yet?"

Seth laughed. "Oh, that. A bunch of times. But you know what I mean. I need some fun before I leave, not drama."

On top of everything, Seth was lying.

"Speaking of which," Seth added. "I have to get Zora for our final goodbye." He laughed.

He was laughing.

"Oh." Razi sounded surprised. "I was talking about Cecile. I had no idea you and Zora were still..."

Zora froze.

"She doesn't know about Cecile," Seth said. "And I'll be far away when she figures it out, which saves me from some dumb drama." He laughed. "Plus I was with Cecile every morning this week. Gets boring."

The only feeling Zora had was a sudden urge to puke.

"Well, have fun, then. I'll see you at your official farewell. Try to leave some girls for me."

"You can have them all. It's not like I'm going to come back and get angry or anything." He sighed. "I hope one day you can get out of this prison, too. For a better future."

"And hotter girls."

Seth laughed. "That, too."

They walked away.

This was like a farce, or more like a weird, strangely written play that made no sense. It made no sense. Zora, who had been leaning on an outer wall of a house, slid down until she was sitting on the ground. This was surreal. Not only did Seth have no intention of coming back, he'd been with another girl. Cecile was nice, about twenty-three. She was a ranger and helped with the rounds to make sure all lights were on. She would be doing that with Seth, except... Perhaps it was logical that there were dark spots so often.

A tear fell on the ground. No. This wasn't right. Seth was the one who had wronged her, perhaps even lied to Cecile, too. Who knew what he had told her? How he'd used his position of "valley hero" to draw on her hope? Stupid hope.

No, not stupid. Zora taught her students hope and bravery. To cower and cry, that wasn't what people in the Dark Valley did.

This was the moment for a quick decision. Zora went back to her house. Her parents were still busy in the treatment room. Did they know Seth was leaving for good? Did they have any idea what Zora had almost done with him tonight? It didn't matter. This wasn't about her parents but about herself.

The right thing to do would be to confront Seth. Right, but pathetic.

Another right thing to do would be to let him spend his last night alone. Another right choice.

But it wasn't what she decided.

2

AN UNFORGETTABLE NIGHT

S eth had a big smile when he opened the door. "For a moment, I thought you had given up. I was almost going to your house to drag you here. I'm not leaving without my gift."

His gift. Oh, dear. How could she have missed these signs?

He looked at her. "You've been crying?"

Zora was annoyed that he could notice it, but she just shrugged, not trying to hide her sadness. "Well, a girl got hurt." Then she showed a wine bottle she had in her hand. "But we also have amazing things to celebrate."

Seth bit his lip. "You know I can't." He didn't seem to have noticed the bag on her shoulder.

Alcohol was forbidden in the Dark Valley, and for good reasons. But her parents had worse potions than that, and wine for medicinal use. At least that was what they claimed.

Zora gave him a sweet, teasing, hopefully seductive smile. "Just a little. You don't need to drink the whole bottle, silly."

Seth took two of the glasses lined up on his counter.

Zora filled her glass, then his, which he tugged down in

one sip, never getting his eyes off her. Quite quick for someone who had said he couldn't drink. And predictable.

Her cup was still in her hand. "Seth, once you win, what are you looking for?"

"Glory. Having my value recognized."

"What about the Dark Valley?" She wondered if he even cared about them, about children getting hurt, about a life in which all they did was get ready to fight and make sure there was light everywhere.

Seth took a deep breath. "I was born for more, Zora, and I'm going to conquer it." He ran his hand over her face. "You'll be my sweet memory. My inspiration. When people sing my name, you'll know you were part of it."

Memory. Were part of it. Zora really hadn't paid attention. "So you're not coming back?" There. She asked.

He paused. "Of course I'm coming back for you." It sounded so fake. Perhaps only now she could see it. Then he smiled. "But you need to encourage me, right? Give me a reason not to forget you."

Zora tried to sound playful, as she put her full glass on the counter. "You're saying that if I didn't come tonight you would ditch me?"

"No. I'm saying that I'm going to find glory and I want you to know that a bit of that glory is yours. You're a girl and all, so you can't do things yourself, but you can be my inspiration. Let's make this night unforgettable."

She considered herself the queen of self-control for not punching him, then looked at him in the eye. "I promise you, Seth. Whatever happens, wherever life takes you, no matter how many years pass, I guarantee you'll never forget this night."

His eyes had that look that she'd always thought was love.

Now she wasn't so sure. He cupped her chin. "You're so perfect."

Before he tried to kiss her, she took his hand and pulled him to the bedroom. "Come. You'll want to lie down."

Seth let her pull him, then push him on the bed, where he sat. Predictable. He smiled at her, the smile she used to think was so sweet, then it was a lazy smile, then his eyes closed and he fell back.

Zora checked his pulse. For a second she feared she'd given him too much sleep grass. But she had counted it right, assuming he'd drink a cup. This wouldn't kill him. She checked his pulse again. Still alive. Yeah, she hadn't given him too much. She exhaled.

Then she checked the lamps in the house to make sure they had enough oil for the night. If a shadow creature spawned inside his house and killed him, what was the point of all that? You can't humiliate dead people.

But everything was fine. Only then she smiled and went back to the kitchen. His bag was ready, everything packed tight so as not to create any shadow. Zora took the letter from the king and a golden rod. They were their champion's trophies, the signs that he'd been chosen to represent the Dark Valley. Except he wasn't going anywhere.

Stupid Seth hadn't even filled his name in the letter. That made things too easy. A good thing she'd packed paper and ink. Zora smiled as she wrote her own name. She then took another piece of paper. Her idea was to write, "Dear Seth, when I find glory, please know that none of it is yours." But then she remembered he couldn't read. She'd wanted to teach him, but he always said reading was useless against shadow creatures and potion ingredients could be memorized. Oh, well.

Few people in the Dark Valley knew how to read. The older people. Zora made her students recite letters and syllables while doing their training routines. Life was about multitasking. And that memory caused a knot in her heart. Her students. But then, she knew she was doing it for her valley, to try to bring help to it. She wasn't like Seth, who was selfish and would forget them. This was her chance to do something for the children. Hopefully. At least she'd come back.

Her parents and her sister needed to know that she was alive and well, but she wasn't going to apologize to anyone. After taking a deep breath, she wrote, "Since Seth was incapacitated to fulfill his duties, I had to step in. I'll be back once I win the competition. As a daughter of the Dark Valley, I have fought since I was a child. I know I can make you all proud."

At least that was what Seth always said, that they were much tougher and stronger and better prepared than anyone else in the kingdom. Zora had faced shadow wolves and even shadow balls. She *taught* children how to face them. A competition against normal people would be a joke. Regardless, the most prominent image in her head was Seth's face waking up and realizing he'd lost his chance at *greatness*. Zora chuckled. Greatness. For someone illiterate and stupid? Ridiculous.

She left the village then walked through the fields towards the inner gate, paying attention that nobody saw her, and also watching in case there was any shadow creature. There were two walls surrounding the Dark Valley, with Gravel soldiers outside. They never opened the gates at night, probably in the mistaken belief that sunlight killed the creatures, so it was unlikely that they would open the gate now. Seth was supposed to leave only in the morning, way past sunrise. His tainted wine should keep him asleep until then. But if it didn't... Stupid note. If he took it to her parents or someone who could read, they'd be after her in no time. If he noticed that the letter and rod were missing... Why was it that ideas were so much more logical in her head?

She hadn't even stepped outside and her plan was falling apart. Her petty, revengeful plan. But it felt so good to be petty and revengeful. She looked at the wall, wondering if she could climb it. Right. As if a bunch of people wouldn't have escaped the Dark Valley by now if they could.

Her only solution was to wait for the sun to rise and hope that Seth slept way past that. Was it wrong to wish for some luck? Just imagining the humiliation if her plan flopped almost gave her a stomachache. And then imagining Seth going to the castle, leaving her and everyone else behind, thinking he was better than them. Better than her. Thinking Zora would be happy to be someone's memory. His memory. Ooooh, what an honor. Thinking she couldn't do anything *because she was a girl and all.*

All his fake words and fake promises came back to her mind, all her thoughts that they had a future together. And she wasn't crazy; he had promised. Empty promises. Better to forget all that. Forget that she'd even accepted to give her body as *a gift.* She was nobody's gift.

Maybe she shouldn't forget. Anger would give her the strength to follow through with her plan. If only anger could make the sun rise earlier. Her eyelids were heavy. Imagine if she fell asleep there?

Perhaps she shouldn't count on luck but on goodwill. She took a look at the letter. It said that the champion should leave in the morning. But then she decided to bet on ignorance.

Zora knocked on the gates. "Guards! Guards! I'm the Valley's champion. I need to leave now. It's past midnight."

No answer. She kept knocking on the metal. So thick. Yet

one shadow ball could finish this. That was why there were two gates. And guards outside.

"It's in the letter," she shouted. "Midnight." She shook the letter. "I'm here and ready to go."

Somebody opened the outer gate. A guard approached. "You were supposed to wait till morning."

Zora shook the letter. "I'm just doing what it says."

He looked at her up and down. "You're the champion?"

She wanted to punch him and his derisive tone. "I happened to kill four shadow wolves at once. They're fast and strong like real wolves. Still think I'm weak?"

He shrugged. "Not saying anything." He was thoughtful. "I'll go and check."

After a few very long minutes, the guard came back with another man, who said, "Let me check the letter."

Oopsies. But then, maybe he didn't know how to read either.

The old man squinted. "It says early morning. Come back later."

Zora took back the letter and feigned sadness and surprise. "Really? I'm so sorry. Our teacher read it, and you know, we don't have time to study, I thought... But I'm here, I said goodbye to everyone. Can you please let me leave now? Just open the gate. There are no creatures close by. You aren't afraid, are you? Please?"

She tried to look at them the way some of her students asked for extra playtime. Zora always said no, but it was for their own good.

The guards looked at each other, then the old men raised the gate just a bit above the ground. "Crawl under it. Quick."

So she had to leave crawling. This wasn't time for pride. Zora was glad to cross the gate, which was shut right after she passed it. Funny how those grown, armed men were terrified of even stepping in the place where she'd always lived.

When they reached the second gate, they opened it enough to allow them to walk through without even crouching.

There were three guards in total. The older guard said, "We don't have anyone to escort you and it's dangerous for a girl to travel alone."

Some exaggeration. "I doubt there will be anything worse than shadow creatures on the road."

He shrugged. "I guess." He then pulled a horse towards her. Zora wanted to run. She'd never been near an animal like that before. But then, it wasn't a shadow creature. He continued, "You need to go to Valerianville. There will be a royal delegation to escort you to the castle. They're lodged at the Oak Tavern and Inn."

"Thanks."

Zora was about to turn and go on her way, when the man said, "Wait. This horse is for you."

Horse. As in riding a horse. She'd probably fall backwards on her first try. But then, she tried to imagine what Seth would do. Would he whine, saying he didn't know how to ride a horse? Oh, no. He'd probably claim he was the best horse rider that had ever ridden. He'd gracefully climb on it and then gallop away. Well, Zora could do that, too. Or maybe she could be rational and prevent a fall and broken limbs.

She smiled. "I'd rather walk. Keep my legs strong."

"Follow the road then, until the crossroad, then turn left and keep going until Valerianville. It's the first town. The Oak Tavern is at the end of the road."

"Thank you." Zora smiled.

These men had given her such a great head start. There

was still kindness in this world, and she had to remember that. And this early departure would give her a lot of time. Even if Seth woke up and complained to the guards, they wouldn't reach her. But then, if he complained, what were the odds they would believe him? Without the letter and the rod? By the time the people from the Dark Valley convinced the guards, if they managed to do that, Zora would be long gone. Once anyone realized the switch, she would already be in the competition. At that point, revealing her farce would only reflect poorly on the Dark Valley.

The most logical thing would be to keep quiet and let her compete. If anything, the person who would need to complain was her father, who acted as the valley representative when dealing with the rest of the kingdom. She had to trust that he wouldn't want to see her fail. She had to trust that he wouldn't want to see her humiliated.

Too late to go back now, and whatever happened, she would manage as best as she could. She knew that part of her was being petty and revengeful like a villain. But villains got away with a lot of stuff. She was counting on that. And loving every moment of giving Seth what he deserved, even if he still wasn't aware of it. No, *especially* because he wasn't aware of anything yet.

It was so strange to walk at night. In the valley, every place would have torches or lamps, and now she was walking on a road surrounded by darkness, only lit by the full moon. Strange how her eyes adjusted and now saw a landscape in shades of grey. A world without color, a world without light, a world she had never before seen. And it took all her strength to keep walking without looking around, Butterfly in hand, ready to take down a shadow creature. There were no shadow creatures outside the Dark Valley, and yet she couldn't erase them from her mind and memory. It was almost strange that people could live like this, walking at night, having their eyes adjust to the dark, without fear.

Zora had the fear, but also the resilience and courage not to let it stop her from going. She wasn't worth less than Seth and she was going to cling to this opportunity to prove it, no matter the cost, no matter how many fears she had to quench and silence. The moment she had put sleep grass in that wine, her decision had been made. It might have been a spur-of-the-moment thing. It might have been fueled by anger and bitterness, but it was done.

After walking through the entire night, Zora's legs were getting wobbly and weak. Perhaps she should have taken the time to learn how to ride a horse. Next time. The worst was that she'd forgotten to bring a snack and her stomach was threatening her with angry growls. Soon it would be morning, and still no sign of any town. Imagine if she took too long to get there, if Seth woke up, and if they sent people after her. Better not imagine that and focus on walking faster. Faster, faster.

The sky was already getting purple when she saw some buildings. Time to find the Oak Tavern. Her legs trembled, and this time it wasn't only because she was tired, but realizing that she was going through with her plan, that she was going to face the royal delegation, that she was indeed, hopefully, on her way to the castle. Well, of course she was. What had all that night walking been for?

There were no buildings with signs. Still, there was a two-storey building right in front of her. Literally at the end of the road, which curved in front of it. Still no signs, but it had to be it.

In the shadow, she saw someone standing in front of the

building. A man leaning on a fence. Arms as thick as her calves, wearing a sleeveless vest even in the cool morning. Maybe he wanted to show off.

Some of Seth's words came to her mind, then, telling her that she was "a girl and all" as if it meant she couldn't do as much as he could. For some reason, the guy reminded her of that, as if he was saying, "Look at me, I'm big and mean, and a man, and oooh, I'm so much better than you."

Perhaps he was mean. Dressed in leathers, it could be a mercenary looking for work somewhere. Maybe an assassin. Well, Zora wore leather too. As she got closer, she realized he was rather young. He had long dark hair parted on the side, covering part of his face with his bangs, and his face was rather nice. Which made no difference. Zora would never notice guys again.

Memories of Seth and of the talk she'd heard kept coming to her mind, her anger bubbling inside, growling in unison with her stomach. She'd never be humiliated again. Ever.

THE COOL NIGHT air felt good on Griffin's bare arms. Outside, alone, below the full moon, he could maybe collect his thoughts. Make sense of what was happening. He leaned on the fence surrounding the tavern, took a sip of his tea, and closed his eyes. It was as if he was a cart on a slope, about to go down faster and faster, each second making it harder to stop, falling from reason, from duty, from everything he'd always valued.

Younger brothers didn't get anything. He shouldn't get anything, and he'd never wanted to take anything from Kiran, his oldest brother. He'd never even envied him, never coveted anything. And yet, there he was, and his mind—and heart— couldn't get over Alegra.

There was no question what his heart wanted, and yet, there was this trace of guilt, this discomfort in the feeling that he was breaching something sacred. But it wasn't as if he could give up on her. Even if he could, it would not change what had already been done.

Griffin should be bursting with happiness. He was. No doubt he was. If only he could quiet his conscience for a while. Kiran would get everything, just not Alegra. Perhaps it was fair.

He took another sip and noticed the sun rising in the horizon, chasing away darkness, its red light warming the colors of the road. Soon it would warm the ground and the air, too. And there was something else on the road. He closed his eyes then looked again, to be sure he wasn't imagining things. He wasn't.

It was as if someone was emerging from the sun. A man. No, too small. A woman. Warrior leathers, a sword on her back, sun-kissed skin, and brown hair with lighter tips, the image looked unreal, as if the goddess of the sun was coming to punish him. Perhaps he deserved it.

As she approached, he realized it was just a girl, shorter than him. Young, too, which didn't explain what she was doing there.

She looked around as if uncertain. "Is this the Oak Tavern?"

Definitely a girl, not a goddess. Griffin had to squint against the sun. "Were you walking alone?"

The girl crossed her arms. "Why? You think I can't defend myself?"

Quite young. Naïve. Overconfident. Very dangerous—for

her. He pointed to the pommel of the sword on her back. "This is cute, but won't save you from—"

Griffin didn't finish as she pulled her sword and in a swift movement, had its tip on his neck.

"Won't save me from what?" she yelled.

He was so stunned that he stepped back, tripped on something, and broke the fence, falling on the mud behind it. He'd been caught off guard. He focused on quieting down the anger menacing to surface. He always had to keep it in check. Without moving, he just stared at her. "Unprovoked violence against an unarmed person. Trying to prove something?"

She still pointed her sword at him. "I have nothing to prove. I'm not weak or lesser than you."

Ha. Words were sharper than steel. "That's in your head, girl. Inferiority complex."

She took a step forward and for a moment he thought he'd have to fight her for real, when he heard the door opening. Oh, no. Alegra.

3

THE PRINCE

Griffin felt mud on his back, and the deep humiliation of having Alegra see him defeated, even if the only reason he was defeated was because this was stupid and he wasn't going to fight a sixteen-year-old. The girl stepped back, as if afraid. Afraid of Alegra. Not Griffin. Some strange world.

"I... I was showing him my sword skills," she said.

Alegra's warm laugh was like calming music cooling down his nerves. "Glad it isn't the other way around," she said. "Come."

She took the girl by the hand and pulled her inside, but not without turning and winking at him. Dangerous game.

HE HAD to carry heavy buckets upstairs to his room, as he didn't want to wake up the servants that early. After filling the tub, he took off his dirty clothes and stepped in. Chilly like the morning. Here he was, bathing in cold water because of his guilt-induced insomnia and then a crazy girl outside. Perhaps cold water would make him go back to his senses. What senses? Alegra here, in this inn, had been a chance meeting, and from chance things had gone this strange and yet wondrous path, one he wasn't sure he could walk away from.

The door opened and he shuddered with the gust of cool air.

Alegra walked in and stood with her hands on her hips. "Taking a bath? That's selfish. Should have invited me."

Griffin shook his head. "It's cold and dreadful."

She took off her shoes, and before he could say anything, stepped in the tub. Not that there was room for two. With a grimace, she said, "You meant it. Cold."

The bottom of her skirt was drenched.

"You're gonna get wet," he warned.

Instead of walking out, she crouched and tilted her head. "Isn't that the whole point?"

He chuckled. "Your clothes are getting wet."

She sat on the tub, so that they were both squeezed there. "Oh, no. My dress will get all wet, then I'll have to wait for it to dry." She rolled her eyes. "So terrible."

Griffin couldn't ignore their closeness, but he also remembered the reason he was there. "I have to go to the Dark Valley."

Alegra put a finger over his mouth. "You're a Gravel prince. You don't *have* to do anything."

Griffin closed his eyes. Prince. Not king. Huge difference there. And there were things he wanted to find out about the Dark Valley. But then Alegra's lips were on his, and his plans didn't matter anymore. All his doubt was gone. In that bath, even his guilt was being washed away. She was no longer Linaria's princess, the hope for an alliance with their kingdom. She was just Alegra.

And he understood. He no longer felt like a cart going down a slope—he'd fallen down a precipice.

Z ora waited at the inn's eating hall. The tables and chairs all had legs and space underneath them, something that would have disastrous consequences in the Dark Valley. There were so many dark spots from where a small shadow spider or ball could spawn and it felt odd to see them and not do anything, to see them and not fear for her life. Strange to feel that even though she was no longer in the Dark Valley, the Dark Valley was still in her.

She ate some bread offered by the owner, who was now busy in the kitchen. Zora had been starving. As the food settled in, her thoughts cleared, and with them, some shame and regret about what she'd done to the guy outside. At least the girl who'd brought her inside didn't seem angry, so that was a relief. Her name was Alegra and she was the most beautiful woman she'd ever seen. Beautiful not like normal beautiful people and beautiful girls in the valley, but beautiful like a heroine in a story, the one everyone fell in love with. She had wavy red hair, light skin, and big dark brown eyes, with perfect features.

And she'd been nice to Zora, even if a bit odd. Their conversation came to her mind.

Zora tried to apologize. "I'm sorry for your friend, I didn't mean it. I was angry, but not at him."

Alegra smiled. "He's not my friend. Nothing to worry about." She chuckled. "And you were right to put him in his place."

Zora was surprised but shook her head. "I didn't mean to hurt anyone."

The red-haired girl raised an eyebrow. "Then perhaps you have to mean it next time. Own it."

Own it. But Zora had been angry at Seth, and the guy wasn't Seth. If she could, she would apologize to him, except that he wasn't outside anymore. Zora didn't want to attack unarmed people who hadn't done anything to her, even if they were obnoxious and underestimated her. For one thing, making random enemies was stupid.

On the other hand, perhaps Alegra could be a good friend. Then, maybe she was a royal and didn't mix with the champions. Zora felt slightly nauseous remembering Razi's words about how people outside were so much better looking than in the valley. Even the rough mercenary-looking guy she'd assaulted was beautiful, when she thought about it.

She closed her eyes. The competition was not about beauty. All that mattered was Zora's skills with a sword, with her mind. Her resilience and courage. She could be uglier than everyone else in the world and it wouldn't make a difference. It shouldn't. Especially considering that she was determined never to fall in love again.

Her sister and her husband came to her mind, with their beautiful kids. Love wasn't all bad. They looked happy. But then she remembered that once she thought that she and Seth would have the same thing, and it all crumbled. So many false hopes. She had to be smarter, that was all. And win the competition.

A blond man with a green velvet vest over a white shirt approached her. He looked at her up and down and raised an eyebrow. "You are the Dark Valley champion?"

Weird how food could change everything. He was looking

at her the way a person checks a dead cockroach, and yet, she didn't feel like punching him or anything, which would be incredibly stupid.

Zora pointed to her bag. "Want to see the letter?"

At least she had that, a written document with her name. Funny that her parents hadn't bothered filling Seth's name. Maybe they were waiting until the last minute, just in case something happened. They were smart—something did happen.

The man waved a hand. "That won't be necessary. Not yet, at least. Why didn't you wait for us? We were going to pick you up in the valley."

"I... wanted... to speed things up? I'm that eager." She smiled.

"Well, you'll need to wait for the prince. He'll check your documents"

Did she hear it right? "P-prince?"

The man rolled his eyes. "He'll be down soon."

As the man walked away, Zora noticed that her heart had sped up. One of the princes was there? In that building? About to see her? And she'd have to lie to him. Well, she'd been doing fine so far. It wasn't that. It was just that she had never imagined that she would see one of the princes up close, that she would talk to a prince.

Which one of them could it be? Gravel had three princes. No, two. One of them had recently been nominated king, after his parents' recent, tragic death. That was Kiran, king at twenty-three. Then there were two younger brothers: Larzen, who, if her memory was correct, was twenty, and Griffin, eighteen or nineteen. As far as she knew, Larzen took care of diplomacy, while Griffin was in charge of the royal guard and everything related to the military. It could be either of them.

And being nervous was stupid. It wasn't as if whoever prince was there would even notice her. It was just... Silly young Zora had always dreamed of one day dancing with a prince. Later she understood that it wasn't a prince that she wanted, but love. Perhaps the idea of a prince came from the stories she read, some unrealistic romantic nonsense that she should have grown out of years ago. No wonder she'd been so naïve. Seth had been her "prince", and look how it had turned out. It had probably been all in her head.

Still, if she ignored all that, meeting a prince meant she was doing something important, that she was someone. Hopefully she wouldn't screw it up the way she'd done this morning, when she had behaved like a brainless shadow creature. And she wouldn't stutter either. Talking to princes was her new normal, now that she was on her way to glory. Weird how that sounded fake when she was thinking it about herself. And she had never doubted it when Seth claimed the same thing.

For all of Zora's anxiety, she ended up not seeing any prince—yet. She tried not to show her disappointment as she was ushered in a carriage with the annoying blond guy. It turned out he was an assistant to the crown, overseeing the competition. His name was Stavos, and she still felt like a cockroach in his presence. It was likely that it would be the same or even worse with either prince. She still had no idea which one of them had been at the tavern, then suddenly had felt "indisposed" and no longer willing to come out of his room. It sounded like an excuse, but she had no idea what for.

Endless fields surrounded the road. A huge world that wasn't encircled in two massive walls. Zora felt free, but at the same time, it was almost as if it was more than she could handle. This insane enormity she could get lost in, a world so big she wasn't sure she could ever find her place there if she tried.

Traveling on a carriage was much better than walking, the soothing sound of wheels and hoofs, and the warm breeze coming from the window easing her fears. With every second, the Dark Valley got further and further behind. With every second, she got closer and closer to the castle. The sound of the carriage was so soothing.

ZORA WAS WALKING ALONE on a path. Only desert around it. Warm sun overhead. A woman with a brilliant crown walked towards her. The Sun Goddess.

"You'll need the Blood Cup," she said.

"For what?"

The goddess smiled. "Don't you know?"

Zora was about to answer "No," when a sudden movement awoke her. Her head was on the carriage seat, her cheek wet from drooling. Weird dream. She didn't believe in gods and goddesses. Maybe as a representation of something greater. Still. And she had never heard of any bloody cup. Zora sat up.

Across from her, Stavos looked out the window. The smell around them was different. It was no longer just nature and earth, but rather food, smoke, people, and even some nasty smells. This was Gravel City, which surrounded the castle. Zora peeked out and saw that they were on a wide street with buildings around it. This was quite different from the valley, where the houses were not close together like that and there were no people selling things on the sidewalk. The valley had no sidewalk either, and certainly no carriages or horses.

Such a multitude on the streets. Then, far ahead, gleaming white towers from the Gravel castle, with golden roofs and turrets. Emotion swelled up on her chest as she realized that yes, she was getting to her destination.

The carriage slowed down as they got closer to enormous metal gates. A girl came to their window, no older than seven or eight, face dirty, wearing rags, her hand stretched. Zora wanted to ask her who she was and what was happening, but the carriage jerked forward.

Zora tapped on Stavo's shoulder. "There's a lost child there."

He stared at her. "And what do you expect me to do?"

Was that a question? "Find her parents. Check if she's hungry."

He waved a hand as if dismissing her. "We can't solve all the problems in the world."

Zora looked back. And the image got clearer. It wasn't just the snobbish blond assistant who was ignoring the girl, but the multitude on the street. How could these people go about their day and not do anything? How could they be so heartless? There were orphans in the Dark Valley, of course. Shadow creatures spared no parents, who, in fact, sometimes died protecting their little ones. When it happened, another family took the child in. Either way, there was always food at the school, and nobody wore rags.

A tear ran down her cheek. She wasn't sure if it was for the child or for the people whose hearts were so cold they could no longer feel compassion. And Zora, without money, means, or anything, felt helpless. Maybe she could find some of these kids, and if they were orphans, bring them to the Dark Valley. And now she was getting all confused because life in the valley wasn't easy either. She'd come thinking of getting more help for her people, and had never imagined that she would see such callousness.

"The child is probably pretending," Stavos said. "They do that to get money from gullible visitors. The mother or father is probably close by, counting the coins they get."

"Oh." That had never come to her mind. "Thanks. For letting me know." It was still upsetting that someone would make a child do that, but perhaps not as terrible as what she had first imagined.

Stavos was looking out the window, but he'd said that for her benefit, so that she wouldn't feel so sad. Perhaps he wasn't that bad after all, and the whole looking at her as if she were an insect was maybe just the way people in the castle behaved. Or maybe it was just her impression.

Fascination, anxiety, hope, eagerness, fear—so many emotions at the same time when they crossed the gates. This wasn't just leaving her valley for the first time, it was going to the castle, being in the most important place in Gravel, and soon at the center of the most important event in the kingdom, a competition only held every three years. No wonder Seth had been so excited about it. Too bad he'd been an asshole to Zora.

With a chill in her stomach, she realized that at this time he must have already woken up. She took a deep breath. The royal delegation was now far from the valley. For Seth to get to her, he'd need to convince the guards at the gates. They'd probably just send a message whenever they could—if they decided to do anything. It wasn't as if one of them would gallop to the castle. Zora had the paper with her name on it. It would be easy to dismiss Seth's allegations as some lunatic's ramblings. If ever these allegations got past the Dark Valley's walls.

The carriage passed the castle yards, then stopped at a building on the back of the castle, some distance from it. Zora followed Stavos through a dark hallway with metal doors leading to bedrooms.

"This is the house of champions," he said. "Simple but comfortable. The idea is that we can keep track of all of you."

They came to a closed door. It had a sign saying "Dark Valley." For some stupid reason, Zora felt emotional, understanding how much she would represent her people.

The blond man opened the door and pointed inside. "There's a bed, a small table, and a water basin. There's a communal bath area, but we'll see what we do about your..." He looked at her up and down. "Specific needs."

Meaning the fact that she was a girl. Which likely meant she was the only female champion.

He continued, "When the prince gets here, we'll see your contract. You can rest now." Pointing to a huge metal bolt, he said, "Always bar the door. We can't guarantee your adversaries won't resort to..." He sighed. "Unethical deeds when away from our eyes."

"I will." Then she smiled. "Thank you."

He had a half-smile that was more like a grimace. "It's my pleasure." Then he turned around and left.

Zora ran to the door and barred it. Unethical deeds. What a thought. It hadn't crossed her mind but made total sense. She wasn't the only one who wanted to win.

Light came from a small, high window with bars. At least she was safe, even though this place looked like a prison. But what bothered her most were the shadows. Dark spaces everywhere. And the covers on the bed. She lifted them and realized the bed was on four legs, with a huge space beneath it. In the Dark Valley, even human shadows would be coming out of there in no time. But this wasn't the Dark Valley. Still, she sat on the bed and couldn't shake the thought that her life would be in danger if she closed her eyes. And yet she was exhausted.

"A GIRL?" Griffin was surprised, as he followed Stavos to the house of champions. He had never considered the possibility that any region wouldn't send a man, but was curious to meet the female warrior. He was then considering the implications. "She'll need new lodgings, then."

"I wasn't given instructions for special accommodations, your highness."

Stavos had a certain bitterness in his tone, as if Griffin had just reprimanded him. He still hadn't gotten used to taking orders from him.

"No," Griffin tried to sound casual. "It's just something that came to my mind now."

"I told her to bar her door."

"Good."

In truth, Griffin's head was far away, still with Alegra.

Stavos knocked on the door with the sign saying "Dark Valley". It had been worth it to miss his visit, and yet, Griffin needed to know more about that place, more about the strange magic creating creatures from the dark. Perhaps it would allow him to understand...

The door opened.

Griffin was stunned. It was the crazy girl from the tavern, sunlight illuminating her hair. Her hazel eyes were wide as she looked from him to Stavos, then put her hand over her mouth. And there was no doubt about her mental state, as he noticed the room. The mattress was on the floor, without covers, and the bed frame had been put up and leaned against a wall. A table was upside down.

He looked back at her. "Nice... decoration you got here. Is there a specific name for this style?"

"Dark Valley." Her voice was apologetic, at least, not confrontational or petulant. "Over there, any dark space will spawn shadow creatures, and I know I'm not there, but I couldn't shake the feeling... I can put it all back." She looked at him, her eyes pleading. "I'm sorry."

Griffin hoped she'd never mentioned their encounter at the Oak Tavern and just smiled. "No need to apologize. I'm in a good mood. Get all your things. Oh. And fix this mess."

The girl started to put her things in a duffel bag.

Griffin didn't want to wait and told Stavos, "Take her to my office."

He walked away trying to think what to do with her. The guests were unlikely to enjoy seeing a cute young girl like that fighting and maybe getting hurt. Insane that the Dark Valley had chosen her, when she was anything but Royal Games material. Now he had to find a solution. Soon.

ZORA WAS FOLLOWING Stavos out of the building. She still didn't know who the dark-haired young man was but had a dreadful feeling.

"Who is he?"

Stavos looked at her for a moment, as if considering an answer, then had sort of a grimace-smirk. "You'll figure it out."

"Why? Is it a mystery or something?"

"No." The man kept walking as if his answer had been enough.

Zora took a deep breath. If the tavern guy was one of the princes, she was neck-deep in trouble. Not only hadn't she addressed him properly just now, this morning's meeting had definitely included a jail-worthy offense. Or worse. In fact, considering that the guy was here in the castle, giving orders, he was obviously someone important, so regardless of who he was, Zora had definitely screwed up big time—and maybe ruined her opportunity.

They entered the castle, and what would have been exhilarating in another circumstance was now terrifying. Zora's palms were sweating and her mind was whirling, trying to come up with a way to explain herself. Unfortunately, nothing acceptable came to her as she passed corridors with tapestries and sculptures, her mind partly admiring their beauty, partly getting spooked by the number of shadows, but mostly dreading her upcoming meeting.

Zora could feel her heart beating when she walked in an almost bare room, with wooden furniture and a fireplace. The wall had swords, shields, axes, and lances, and she couldn't help but admire their craftsmanship. The guy from the tavern was sitting on an armchair, a booted leg on a small table, his eyes looking down at the leather bands around his wrist as if uninterested.

The door closed, and Zora realized Stavos had left. She was alone with the mysterious guy, her heart almost exploding.

"Please, sit." His tone was icy and he still fumbled with leather straps on his wrist, but when she sat, he raised his dark eyes to her. At least she didn't feel like an insect, but rather like a target he was planning on throwing something at.

He raised his eyebrows. "Satisfied? Got a kick out of overwhelming a prince?"

As she feared. And that had to be Griffin, the youngest. She wished the ground would open and she could fall through a hole below her. But she couldn't, so she had to say something. "I'm truly sorry. I know it's not a valid excuse, but I was super hungry. And angry. At someone else. And I had no idea you, uh, your highness was one of the princes, not that it excuses what I did, but I swear I felt bad right—"

He raised a hand as if to silence her. "I already forgot it, and I suggest you do the same. Let's put this incident behind us." His eyes were piercing.

A glimmer of hope was lit in her heart. Of course. Would he want to tell people that he had fallen in the mud? Of course not. And she had no intention of ever mentioning it.

Zora smiled. "Thank you."

Griffin leaned back on the chair, eyes still on her, making her tremble. "This is a special time for Gravel. A time for festivities, celebration. I was the one who insisted on having a representative from the Dark Valley, and I'm glad you're here. We have visitors from the entire kingdom and from abroad, including nobles and rich merchants. This festival is not only about the Royal Games, but an opportunity for the youth of our kingdom to..."

He took a deep breath and closed his eyes. "Find their ideal partners. In this condition, you'll be placed in the castle and you'll be part of all the festivities. I'm confident you'll find a great match."

Match? As in getting married? Zora blinked, and when no other possibility came to her mind, she shook her hands in front of her. "No, no, no. I don't do the whole... matching thing. I gave that up. I just want... to win the competition. That's all."

He glared at her for a second. "All? That's it? As if it were nothing? As if there weren't eleven more seasoned warriors plus me wanting the same thing? As if you stood a chance?"

That wasn't true. "I *have* a chance."

Griffin rolled his eyes and she grabbed the arms of the chair with all her strength to prevent her hands from doing something stupid.

He got up. "The Royal Games..." He paused while running his hand through his hair, revealing a long sideburn that she hadn't noticed until then. "Is not a competition against unaware, unarmed adversaries."

Zora got up as well. "I'm from the Dark Valley. I bet you have no idea what I've faced before. What I can face. I can fight."

"I'm not doubting that. It's just... This year is special, it's not the normal games, it's the Blood Cup, and it will be dangerous."

Blood Cup? The name rang a bell. The goddess. He'd gotten her attention.

"It's important for many reasons," he continued. "But it's also entertainment for our visitors. People might get hurt, and it will still be entertaining. I do hope nobody dies, but if a champion does, the crowds might still love it. But nobody is coming to Gravel to see a pretty girl risking her life in the arena."

She'd been so caught up wondering what this Blood Cup was that his words didn't make sense at first, until she realized he was talking about her. Griffin, the handsome youngest Gravel prince was saying Zora was pretty. And yet she felt horrible.

She stepped close to him. "That wasn't in the instructions we were sent." She knew it because she'd read them. "We were supposed to choose our best, our strongest. I *earned* my place." That was a lie, but he didn't need to know. "What are you going to tell my people? How will they feel when they're told they're out of the Royal Games?"

He put his hands on her shoulders, in a gesture that felt patronizing. "There's still time to bring someone else from your valley. You can stay for the festivities. Take part in the balls, the celebration, find allies, maybe even a husband."

"I don't want to get married!" she yelled, then realized she was breaching decorum again. "Your highness," she added in a low voice.

At least he stopped touching her and crossed his arms. This was like Zora's worst nightmare. Seth would then be back in the competition and would humiliate her. She sat down again, and to her horror, realized that tears were forming in her eyes. In a way, the prince was humiliating her, too, telling her that the only thing she was good for was to serve a man, as if she were only an object, nothing more.

Griffin crouched in front of her, his expression calmer. "See? That's the problem. You cry like that and I feel bad for what I said. But imagine if you get hurt. I'm considering our guests and visitors, but I'm also considering your own well-being."

Zora felt so worthless, so powerless. And even worse that he was using her tears as a reason to get her out of the games. Then a thought came to her, quick as lightning: Seth wouldn't be crying and feeling sorry for himself. He'd stand up proud and demand his right to be part of the Blood Cup. She didn't have to accept it either.

She gave him an icy smile. "That's all great. Change the rules for *next* time. For now, I won my right to be here fair and square." She pulled her bag and showed him the letter. "My name is here: Zora Sunborn, and it was the choice of the Dark Valley according to *your* rules."

He smiled, unfazed. "My rules. Exactly. And I can change them."

Something came to her mind. "Didn't you say you were competing? Your highness." She really had to get better at using these titles.

"What's the difference?" He raised an eyebrow.

"Maybe your highness is afraid of getting your high ass kicked." His eyes had a dark glint. She took some courage and smiled. "Again."

He stared at her for a moment, then burst out laughing. "No. That's certainly not the case."

She ignored his laughter. "Then you have nothing to lose. If I'm weak like you think, I'll be out in the first round. If I'm not, then what's the problem? People will realize I'm a competitor like the rest, a person, not just a cute little pretty thing that's only good to serve men."

"I never meant that." He got up suddenly, frowning and looking as offended as if she said he ate puppies for lunch.

She narrowed her eyes. "Then what did you mean?"

Griffin stared at her as if thinking. She'd nailed it. Then there was a knock on the door and it opened.

A handsome young man stepped in. He had dark blue eyes and brown hair with some braids with blue beads on the bottom and wore a satin white overcoat and dark blue velvet pants.

"Brother?"

So that was either King Kiran or prince Larzen.

The newcomer then smiled. "I had no idea you had female company or else I wouldn't have—"

"This is the champion the Dark Valley sent." Griffin closed his eyes, as if annoyed.

"Oh. Lovely." The newcomer approached Zora, knelt on one knee, took her hand, and kissed it. "Prince Larzen."

Zora was so stunned it took a while for her to reply. "An honor, your highness. I'm Zora Sunborn."

He got up and smiled. "Born from the sun indeed."

It didn't make her feel good. She didn't want them reminding her she was a girl, and then telling her she couldn't compete. "I'm a fighter, too. I've been facing shadow creatures since I was a little girl."

"No doubt," the prince said. "Or you wouldn't have been selected for the Blood Cup."

"Larzen." Griffin's voice was a warning and he shot Zora a look that pierced like a sword. "I don't think she's a good fit for it. We were working on a solution."

"I earned my place in this competition," Zora insisted.

"And you should be proud." Larzen smiled. He turned to Griffin. "Our rules never stated that only men should compete. Wasn't it you who decided to allow women in the army? In the Royal Guard?"

"Strong fighters. Or archers, doctors, strategists, not—"

Larzen waved a hand. "She'll do fine. Or not. But that's not up to us to decide. If she's the champion they sent us, we must trust that they knew what they were doing. I think our guests will love her."

Griffin crossed his arms and looked away. "Whatever, then." He stared at her. "If you get hurt, I don't want to see a single tear."

Zora could also shoot daggers from her eyes. "You won't."

"She'll need special accommodations, right?" Larzen asked.

Griffin nodded while rolling his eyes.

"I'll take care of it," the older prince added. He then turned to Zora. "Follow me."

As Zora followed Larzen through more and more corridors, she could barely believe that the worst was over, that she was in the competition, that Griffin didn't want to imprison or execute her for what she'd done in the morning. She was still hurt by his words saying that she should look for a husband instead of fighting, though.

But on the bright side, she was walking with a prince, a real prince, like the ones she'd dreamed about. Not that she wanted anything romantic with him, but it still was like a wish coming true. Griffin, on the other hand, didn't give her the same impression, didn't feel like a prince. This morning she'd thought he was some kind of mercenary, now she thought he was an annoying hurdle on her way.

They entered a room, but this had two beds, rugs, and a big window with curtains. It wasn't anything like the prison-like room from the house of champions. There was a suitcase already in a corner and one of the beds was unmade. So many dark spots Zora wanted to jump at, except that she had to control herself.

"You'll share a room with Loretta." Larzen pointed inside. "She's from Gold Port and I think you'll like her."

"That's great. Thanks."

He was chuckling, then. "You got some talent, girl." He mimicked her voice: "I earned my place in this competition." He bent down laughing. "Even I almost believed you."

Zora felt the blood drain from her face but didn't think he'd notice it considering how tanned she was. She smiled as if confused. "I don't understand."

He pointed to her. "Excellent, that's what I'm talking about."

She tilted her head. "Are you, erm, is your highness going to explain what's so funny?"

He took both of her hands in his. "No highness, dear. Just Larzen. My dear prince works, too. I'm your friend. So much your friend that I didn't tell my lovely brother that you're an impostor."

4

THE OTHER PRINCE

Zora kept her face blank, just a little surprised. "Where did you get that idea?"

Larzen laughed. "Girl, you're good. Now, the thing is, we got letters from all the regions. In the case of the Dark Valley, their champion wasn't a girl."

She wasn't going to quit that easily, she had to keep fighting. She shrugged. "Of course. I placed second. Our champion got ill the night before he was supposed to come." It was always a good idea to keep the lie close to the truth.

"Interesting." He raised his eyebrows. "And you wouldn't have anything to do with this mysterious, sudden, illness?"

Illness. That was a brilliant idea that hadn't crossed her mind, but she just laughed. "Why? You'd think I'd knock on the champion's door offering a drink and he'd take it? Who would be that stupid?"

"No idea. Had that been the case, I wouldn't hold that against you, just so you know. You get to places in life with brains. But I guess I'll apologize for my wrong assumption, then."

She shook her head. "No need. It's understandable." She still wasn't sure if he believed in her or if he was just pretending.

"I still want to be your friend." He sat on a bed. "Tell me, what is it you want?"

"To win the competition."

He narrowed his eyes. "Is it, though? Because you see, people go on and on saying 'I want this, I want that,' when in fact what they truly mean is 'wouldn't it be nice if this or that happened?' Words are easy. It's easy to say you want something. It's easy to convince yourself you want something. The hard part is to do whatever it takes to get it, to commit to getting it. That's the part everyone skips. On which side are you?"

Zora stepped back. She hadn't even given it that much thought. All that she wanted was to prove herself, avenge Seth, and get help for her people. Then she imagined herself coming home empty-handed, imagined the disappointed looks in her family, friends, students. Imagined they would think she stole their opportunity. "I need to win."

"You need to win. Hum, interesting. Shouldn't you *be certain* you're going to win?" Otherwise you have already lost."

He had a point. Seth spoke as if he'd already won the games, but then, perhaps that was idiocy, too. "What difference does it make? I bet most of the competitors think they are going to win this thing. It doesn't mean they will."

"That's a naïve thought, Zora. Some of them only hope to do well, some hope to get as far as possible. Some of them *wish* they could win. I would bet anything that the only person who truly sees himself holding the Blood Cup is my younger brother."

"Which is unfair, if he's helping to organize the competition."

Larzen had a smirk. "Life is unfair, isn't it? Do you understand what the winner of this competition gets?"

"Some money, and a place at the royal guard, if we want it."

"Hum... Do you know what the Blood Cup is?"

"The... special name for the competition this year." To be very honest, she'd heard it for the first time today.

Larzen smiled. "It's a red cup. It can only be given to the winner of this competition. I'm not sure what it's made of. Crystal? But that's not the point. The thing is, you can brew potions in it."

That got her interest. "Special potions."

"Who knows? With the cup's unique magic maybe you could find a solution for your valley."

"What about the previous winners? Haven't they used it? Is there a new cup made every now and then?"

"You need to win the competition to be able to use the Blood Cup. As to the previous winners, sadly, they all died. The Blood Cup demands a sacrifice and its last challenge might be difficult, or rather, quite deadly. That's the reason this competition hasn't been held in the last twenty-seven years. Why we just called the competition Royal Games and didn't put the cup as a prize. But this year it's the Blood Cup."

Zora was thoughtful. "Griffin wants this cup."

Larzen smiled. "Exactly."

Something didn't make sense. "Wouldn't you rather he got it?"

He raised his eyebrows "Would I?"

Zora tried to think. Perhaps there was rivalry among the brothers?

Larzen laughed. "I'll be honest. I don't care who wins this

45

thing. I just need a friend. So here's my deal. I can help you win this competition, Zora. But you'll need to be my friend." He took her hand.

Zora tensed. "And do what?" Larzen was extremely good looking, but she wasn't sure if she'd be willing to do anything for his help.

"What?" He laughed, then let go of her hand. "Please. You think I need to beg or coerce anyone for some nice moments? Look at me. And more, most of the fun is in your partner's enthusiasm. It takes two, right? I mean, two minimum." He put a hand on his chin and looked up. "But then, there's the solo thing too. Not sure it counts. It also needs enthusiasm." He looked at her. "I can see you know nothing about it."

Duh. She knew the solo thing, not that she wanted to discuss it with him. Zora crossed her arms. "What do you want?"

"Goodness, you put it as if it were a cold exchange of services or goods. I want friendship, cooperation. And I'll help you get your hands on the cup."

"I might be able to win on my own." She wasn't that confident, to be honest, but didn't want to bend that easily.

"I thought you were smart. You haven't seen your competitors, have you?" He didn't wait for a reply. "They all have teams helping them, strategists, trainers, spies. Nobody ever achieves anything on their own, even if they are selfish and make sure history registers only their name. Go on this competition alone, and you'll be doomed. Might is not good enough, dear."

"Only the champion was allowed out of the Dark Valley, though. Of course I don't have a team."

"Cause my brother's a nitwit. Not that he did it on purpose. But he set you up for failure. Or he never thought the Dark Valley would send a serious contender. It was an empty gesture; allow one of you to partake in the competition, as if to say, 'look how nice I am, allowing this poor competitor to even stand among our best.' I doubt he thought a Dark Valley champion had a chance."

The idea stung. Zora looked down. "He's stupid, then."

"No doubt. But you shouldn't play his game. Get that cup." He laughed. "I'll confess that part of me just wants to see his disappointed face."

"I wouldn't mind that either." Zora was smiling as she imagined it. She wasn't sure she trusted Larzen, but hearing what he had to say couldn't hurt. She then tried to word her request in a way that wouldn't bother him. "But friends are honest with each other, and I would like to know how I can help you."

"There's something you said that stuck with me. When Griffin was suggesting you partake the festivities, you said you didn't do the whole matching thing."

She frowned. "You weren't in the room then."

Larzen shook his head and sighed. "That thin door! We really need to fix it. But this was important to me. Not sure you realized, but the Blood Cup isn't the only game we're having for the annual festivities. There's the courting game. I need a female player to support me. One that has no stakes in it."

"What would you want me to do?"

"Nothing much. Certainly not have any fun with anyone. I wouldn't ask you that. In fact, getting physical too early kind of spoils the game, you know? All I'll need is for you to, I don't know, talk to someone, get their attention. You don't need to be something you're not. A Dark Valley competitor uninterested in dating or marriage is quite perfect. You'll go to balls, maybe walk in the garden or other places, and I'll nudge you here and there. I'll also get you dresses."

"Dresses?"

"How do you expect to go to balls?"

Dresses would create shadows right between her legs. Nobody wore any kind of loose clothing in the Dark Valley. But she was no longer there and had to smarten up. "I was just surprised."

"So in short, that's it. You'll get some beautiful dresses and will go to the royal balls. Griffin already agreed to that. Then if I ask you to talk to someone, go in a certain direction... It's not the end of the world, is it?"

"I need to be sure you'll really help me."

"No question about it. If my instructions don't help you pass a task, you can stop helping me. If you no longer help me, I'll stop giving you instructions. We won't even need to trust each other."

"Sounds good. It's a deal, then."

"If you need me, tell your attendant. But you won't be alone. I put you here with Loretta for a reason. You might get a note from me from time to time. Come and meet me, then. And never aim low. Want that cup. I'll do all I can for you to get it. But you have to want it." His gaze was intent on her.

Zora smiled. "Don't worry about it."

Larzen nodded and left.

She wasn't exactly sure if she should trust him and if he was truly going to help her win the competition. But there was something else, too. One of her goals was to get more help and support for the Dark Valley, and getting close to the prince who dealt with diplomacy could only be useful.

And he was right that she needed to want the cup and be confident she could get it. No more settling for less, settling for just enough, settling for second. She'd gone this far tricking, lying, and not playing by the rules, and there was no reason to stop being smart now. Zora was a decent fighter, but not the best, fastest, or strongest. Still, she had her mind. She could read, she could think, she could brew potions—and she'd better use all her talents.

Zora sat on the bed trying to trick her mind into stopping worrying about shadows. It had been ingrained in her from an early age. The ability to prevent dark spots was even more important than knowing how to fight. If ever a dark creature spawned in your bedroom when you were deep asleep, skills would be unlikely to save anyone's life.

But now she had to reconsider pushing beds against the wall, especially now that she would share the room with someone. Griffin's mocking face and comment when he'd seen her room in the house of champions were fresh in her mind, and made her feel small. Well, if she won the cup instead of him, she'd be the one with the mocking face. Simple solution. Complex execution.

Then Zora's stomach's started rumbling. It was already three in the afternoon, meaning she'd slept a whole lot—and missed lunch. She was trying to figure out what to do when a young woman stepped into the room. She was about nineteen, with dark hair pulled up in a complex hairdo, light skin, curvy with soft features and a warm smile.

"Are you Loretta?" Zora asked.

"Why, yes." The girl locked Zora in a tight hug, then looked at her. "I assume we'll share the room."

"If it's not a problem."

Loretta laughed. "Problem! I asked for a friend. You think I want to be alone here, staring at walls? Plus, what's the fun in flirting if we don't have anyone to talk to? What's your name, dear?"

"Zora. I'm from the Dark Valley. I'm one of the champions."

She looked at her up and down. "Wow, impressive. I would never have guessed it. You're lucky. They're saying the competitors this year are looking more than fine."

"I haven't met them yet." She didn't want to be rude and cut the conversation, but there was no way she would be able to continue being civil without some food first. "Do you know where I can eat, or if I have to call someone or do something?"

Loretta pulled Zora's hand, and soon they were speeding through hallways until they came to a gigantic kitchen with ovens on one wall, a line of stoves in its middle, and people working on counters.

They sat at a table by a corner, while someone gave Zora some soup and bread. There were no leftovers from lunch, and it was too early for dinner. Loretta knew the assistants working there, which helped a lot. She was talkative and funny, and was a shop owner who'd come to the festival to meet people, or rather, meet interesting men. From her talk, Zora assumed that the competitors were also seen as husband material. She wondered if Seth had known. No. Zora had read all the communication from the castle, and it was just about sending a strong, young warrior to partake in the triannual games. Nothing about matchmaking. Nothing even about this bloody cup.

"You look sad, dear," Loretta interrupted her thoughts.

"Just thoughtful."

"Are you finished?"

Zora nodded.

Loretta got up. "I know what you need, then! A bath."

The woman took her back to the bedroom, where they got their things, then to the women's baths. Zora memorized the passages and the ways so that she wouldn't need help every time she needed something simple. The bathhouse had several curtained sections and attendants filling them with hot water. That was something Zora also needed, after having walked so much.

As they got back to their bedroom, Zora asked, "How do you know prince Larzen?"

Loretta widened her eyes. "Larzen?" She lowered her voice. "Prince Larzen? I don't know him personally. Wouldn't mind it, frankly. He's a sight to behold, isn't he?"

"Yes. It's just... He's the one who got me this room. He said he put me with you on purpose."

Loretta threw her head back and laughed. "You're joking, right?"

"No."

"Well, I'm insanely flattered. All I did was ask Tania, our attendant, to send me a roommate. I never thought..." Loretta touched her arm. "So you *spoke* to him?"

"Just stuff about the cup." Zora didn't want to seem like she was close to the prince or something.

The woman waved a hand. "Oh, right. You champions and your privileges. You'll have to help out a girl looking for love."

Zora smiled. "I'll try."

Someone knocked on the door. Loretta ran to it, and hugged a small, dark-haired girl of about fifteen or so, then turned to Zora. "This is Tania, our little wish granter."

"I'm Zora."

The girl nodded and smiled. "The champion. I know. I'm just here to tell you that you need to be at the back of the arena at six. The champions will be presented tonight."

Zora felt her heart speeding. Six? There was a clock in the room, and it was already four. She could barely believe that in about two hours her farce was about to become real. This was all becoming real. There was a mix of natural apprehension about being in front of so many people, plus the small fear that someone would find out her deception, that somehow Seth would find a way to expose her. And yet what she felt most was the satisfaction of enjoying something that had been meant to be his. He shouldn't have messed with her. Annoying Griffin felt good, too.

Tania turned around to leave, but Loretta yelled, "Where do you think you're going?"

"I..." The girl was surprised.

Loretta laughed and took a coin from her purse. "Never leave without your gold." She put it on the girl's hand.

Tania smiled and left. When the girl was gone, Loretta said, "Spending on loyalty is never a waste."

"I'm doomed, then." Which was true. Zora didn't have a single coin. Perhaps there had been some in Seth's bag, but she hadn't looked for that.

"Don't be silly. Money is not the only currency in the world."

Zora didn't want to consider what other currencies there were. She needed some time to collect her thoughts, and then she remembered a detail prince Larzen had told her; that nobody had ever won the Blood Cup. This wasn't something to be ignored. With still an hour before having to get ready to go to the arena, Zora decided to do something useful.

"Do you know if there's a library in this castle?"

Loretta looked disappointed. "Are you sure? We could go to the gardens. It's the best place to, you know, see and be seen. Although, I guess you don't need to worry about being seen. I'll take you there but I won't stay."

"No problem." Zora smiled. Her one goal was to win that competition, and if she truly wanted to achieve that, she'd need to spend every waking hour working towards it. And getting more information about it was a great first step.

They walked to a huge golden door.

"Thank you so much," Zora took Loretta's hands in hers. "For everything you did today. It would have been lonely, confusing, and awful without you."

"Nah. It's my honor to help you. Enjoy your books but don't get lost in them. I'll cheer for you tonight."

Zora laughed. "At least one person will."

"I'll be the first of many, you wait and see."

Loretta turned around and disappeared in the hallway. Funny how Zora had even stopped looking for dark places. It was as if Loretta's calm and cheerfulness had been contagious. Prince Larzen had indeed made a good choice. So far he'd been keeping his side of the bargain. Hopefully her part wouldn't be hard.

Zora took a deep breath. Such a huge door for just a library. She pushed it hard and it swung inward quickly, being much lighter than what she'd predicted. As she stepped in, she had to catch a breath. Not even in her dreams she'd have imagined a place like this.

It was a circular room with a window on the roof from which sunlight came in. There were shelves from the floor to the top, and three mezzanines for the higher books. Even then, some books would still require ladders. On the ground floor, there were three more doors, which certainly led to even more sections in this library.

In the Dark Valley, her house had been the one with most books; an entire wall, with topics ranging from poetry and stories to potion ingredients, anatomy, and some history. Zora had read many of those books twice. The school also had a full wall with books. That was what she'd imagined when considering a library.

But this, this was too much. She wasn't sure she'd be able to read all those books even if she did nothing else for her entire life. It was more than what a single person could ever learn, could ever absorb, so much knowledge and art, and who even knew what else? It was part dream and part agony as she contemplated her own human limitation. Study as she might, she'd never even come close to the knowledge in a single library in a single castle in a single kingdom. And yet, there were probably so many wonderful things she could learn! Potion recipes, more healing herbs, maybe she'd even find answers to the Dark Valley, maybe even a solution for them.

Her eyes were misty as she looked up in awe, contemplating the beauty and power in that single room, thankful for the opportunity of being there, amazed at the beauty of the library.

Then, for a brief second, she felt a chill in her stomach, and looked down from the books to find intent dark eyes on her. Griffin leaned on a door.

5

AWE AND WONDER

Zora shuddered.

Griffin stood straight. "I take it you can read?"

"Well... Why else would I be here?"

He shrugged. "No reason, of course. Reading and research-ing. That's all people do in libraries. Certainly." His tone was weird, as if he were explaining himself or confused, talking a little too fast.

Zora smiled. "Turns out I'm not *that* useless."

"Absolutely." He walked towards her. "Which is one more reason you shouldn't be competing. This competition, it's physical. Most of the champions are latching on to their only shot at achieving something. It's the only thing they can do. That's not your case." He was right in front of her now, at an arm's reach, not that she would ever reach an arm towards him.

"Aren't you also competing? And yet, your highness obvi-ously can read, or else you wouldn't be here."

He sighed. "My case is different. If it helps, I wouldn't want either of my brothers fighting for this cup either. It's not because you're a girl, it's just because I don't think it's for you."

"Why are you in it, then?"

"Personal reasons. But I'm sure you didn't walk into this library by chance. I can help you. What are you looking for?"

Zora almost made up a stupid excuse for being there, but maybe it was better to make her commitment clear. "Historical records. Information about previous Blood Cups."

"That's an excellent idea. Perhaps the written word will be more persuasive than me and help you come to your senses. Follow me."

He entered a door. Zora was surprised to come to another room with books, but this wasn't as tall and had only a few rows of shelves. On a corner, there was a metal door. Griffin opened it, revealing a small room with a round table in the middle and shelves with old, worn books on two walls. There were no windows in this room, which was lit just by a lamp on the table.

This was more like her library at home.

He pointed at the shelves. "Here we have records about the triannual competitions. Not all of them were for the Blood Cup, but I'm sure you'll find whatever you're looking for. If you ever want to research a specific subject, come in the morning, when we have a librarian on duty. But this should help you for now."

Zora was actually surprised that he'd helped her. "Thank you." Then she added, "I'm not going to give up the competition, though."

He stared at her for a moment, then sighed. "I suggest you do. Just don't show up tonight. And you'll still be welcome to partake in the festivities. If you want to help your valley, you need to be doing politics. That happens in the ballrooms, dining rooms, even gardens. Not the arena."

"I'll do both."

"As you wish." He rolled his eyes and left.

Right. He was quite delusional if he thought she was going to give up. Now, onto what mattered; information.

Zora was unsure from where to start, so she pulled a book at random. The title was "Triannual festivities: Year 33". That had been seven hundred years before. It was surprising that the book was still intact. Maybe it was a copy. Gravel counted the years dating from when their kingdom had been formed. Year 33 was even before the Dark Valley. She would need to comb these books for when the festivities had the Blood Cup but she didn't even know when they chose to hold that celebration instead of the regular festivities. Perhaps this would be easier to do in the morning, when they had a librarian. She moved to the far right and bottom of the shelf, trying to find one about the celebration from twenty-seven years before. The book she pulled was from year 3. The years were not in order.

Perhaps this was a deposit of what they considered worthless material. Was Griffin playing tricks on her? Well, not really, this room *did* have information about the Royal Games, it was just that it was disorganized.

And there was no clock in it. Perhaps she'd better come back later, with time to really dig through the records, without worrying about being late. She should also ask Prince Larzen for everything he knew, writing down dates. That would be a better starting point. She sighed and went to the door. Weird. Zora could swear it had been left open. Or maybe she was confused.

No wonder, for some reason meeting Griffin stressed her. Perhaps it was still the fear that he would sentence her to death or prison for having attacked him, or the very real possibility that he would come up with a convoluted rule to keep her out of the competition. It was even hard to focus.

Zora turned the handle, but the door didn't move. Then she tried turning the handle differently, pushed the door really hard, and it still didn't budge. She tried a few times and got no result. Horror struck her as she realized she'd been locked in. She banged on the door.

"Hello! Someone! Open up!"

On the back of a huge library on a remote corner in the castle, she'd have to yell a lot. Zora wanted to strangle herself. How stupid she'd been following Griffin, thinking he was being helpful. No wonder he'd been calm and even polite. His plan was to sabotage her odds at getting the cup. Zora hated him.

After struggling against the handle some more, she kicked the door and only managed to hurt her foot. No. She had to think. Think what? It wasn't as if breaking down a door was among her skills. Being stupid, on the other hand, was right there on top. There wasn't a lock for a key, which meant that there was something outside keeping the door locked, probably some kind of bar. Groaning in frustration wasn't going to help.

Then, from bad, her situation suddenly turned to worse, as the lamp went out. This wasn't like when she walked at night and the moon and stars changed the landscape to tones of grey. This was complete blackness. No difference between eyes open or closed. She pulled her sword from her back. It had a subtle pink glow, not enough to allow her to see anything other than her sword.

She felt that at any moment something would jump on her, and having her sword ready eased some of her fear. Still, her heart beat very fast and she turned around to cover every direction, but nothing came towards her. Zora sheathed her sword, sat on the floor, and took slow, deep breaths. Yes, everything was dark, but she was safe, nothing was going to attack her. She was safe, she was safe, there was nothing in that room.

After a few minutes, she got up. This was not the time to be scared or to berate herself. It was time to act. Yelling was pointless. Her voice didn't have that much reach, and had a limit, too. What she had to do was one of two things: either force the door open or make enough noise to alert someone.

Stepping carefully, she reached out her hands in front of her until she touched the table, then pushed it towards the door, pulled it a bit, then kicked it with all her might. Bam. That was more noise than yelling. She didn't even need to pull the table much, as the impact pushed it back from the door. All she needed to do was push it or kick it with all her might, and let its weight hit the door, a strong thud reverberating through the room, hopefully through the library, and perhaps reaching the hallways outside. Perhaps it would even force the door open.

Again and again, she pushed it at about every thirty seconds, to the point her body hurt and sweat dripped from her forehead. It was strange to be in this completely dark place, but at least her fear and apprehension were gone, replaced by anger. All she had to do to keep going was imagine she was kicking or pushing Griffin. It turned out that she'd been right to push him to the ground on their first meeting. And now she was pushing a table. And all the noise she was making had no effect whatsoever. What kind of people were these who left such a majestic library empty, abandoned?

She lost track of time and had to fight back tears, when she finally heard someone outside asking, "Zora?"

"Here! I'm locked! Open the door."

After a loud screech from the door, Tania was outside, breathless, holding a candle that looked bright as sunlight. "I was looking for you everywhere. You have to run or you'll be out."

"Which direction?"

"Right at the hallway to the front gate, then down the hill."

Zora was out the door not even a second later, running as if ten shadow wolves were after her and her life depended on her speed. She'd practiced running a lot in the Shadow Valley, and taught it, too. It was the easiest way to survive a human shadow or even a ball, sometimes even shadow wolves depending on their distance. Even experienced rangers sometimes had to run when outnumbered. And with that thought, she dashed to the back of the arena. Breathless and confused, she stared at three different doors, until someone pulled her hand. It was Stavos.

"Silly girl, what were you thinking? You missed the rehearsal."

Zora was so out of breath she couldn't even respond, and plus she was actually glad he was pulling her somewhere. It meant it wasn't all lost. He led her to a small door, then said, "Follow them."

In front of her, a line of men were walking into the arena. Zora ran and stood at the end. They walked to a place that had a semi-circle drawn on the ground, around a pyre. Zora was at one end of the semi-circle, and Griffin at the other. He frowned when he saw her. She stared at him as if saying, "I know what you did and you'll regret it."

It didn't seem to bother him, as he moved his eyes away

from her and looked at the stands, as if searching for someone. The stands. Holly light. So many people that it was impossible to count them, impossible even to find anyone. Zora wondered if Larzen was there. On the lower part of the stands there was a section with glass windows and a golden roof, probably made for special guests and even the royal family, but she couldn't see across the glass.

A loud thud scared her, then she looked at the sky and realized there were fireworks forming figures as if the stars had been brought close to them. Then they formed flowers and circles, and her jaw dropped when she saw a line of interconnected forms at the same time. A brilliant painting in the sky.

Then some people ran onto the stage, men and women wearing tight-fitting clothes, some of them juggling, some doing acrobatics. At a corner, there was an orchestra playing, with string instruments and drums. The only music they had in the valley was singing and some wind-up music boxes, the internal gears packed tightly not to form big, empty spaces. They also had harps and flutes, but the knowledge of how to play them had been lost generations ago. Other instruments required hollow dark parts that were not allowed in the valley.

Listening to these for the first time, seeing the musicians turn movements into harmonious sound, brought tears to her eyes. This was so much more than the music boxes. Then there were the acrobats and dancers. They were now standing on each other, and then others standing on their shoulders. The top ones jumped and came down as if rolling in the air. She had no idea people could do that. Technically, she had read about acrobats, but still, it was different to see them in real life, right in front of her.

The crowd erupted in applause, and she applauded, too. One of the acrobats knelt in front of her and extended a hand with a yellow flower. She took it and put it behind her ear. It was just a flower, but she was emotional with the gesture.

Then she got a weird feeling, like a gust of chilly air. From the corner of her eye, she saw Griffin staring at her. She didn't care. And she didn't care if people saw her crying. She'd promised not to cry if she got hurt, and well, she wasn't hurt. This was her first time hearing instruments and seeing acrobats and she wasn't going to waste effort trying to pretend it didn't touch her. Plus, it should be more than obvious that those were tears of joy, marvel, awe, wonder, and appreciation. Zora loved to be there, to see all that. She was going to do everything it took to deserve that honor. To honor her valley.

Someone pushed a cage with a lion in it. She felt sad that the cage was small, but this was probably just to show the animal in the arena. It looked like a cat, and she wished she could pet him. Of course, she couldn't and she wouldn't, but it was amazing to see such a beautiful, graceful creature from up close.

A man with a golden suit then entered the stage and the music quieted down. He held a golden cone in front of him to amplify his voice.

"Welcome, everyone! These are your champions! They represent honor, strength, resilience, and let's not forget, the union and harmony among all corners of our kingdom!"

And yet, up until then, apparently it had been as if the Dark Valley didn't exist.

The man had a paper with names, walked towards her, but then moved to the champion to her side and presented him. It was a blond young man with brown skin and green eyes, dressed as if about to go to a party, not a competition. In fact, she took a look at them. They were all young and many of them were rather good looking. At this point, she'd seen enough people in the city, tavern, and castle to know that they didn't all look like Griffin or Alegra. She disagreed that people in the rest of the kingdom were much better looking than in the Dark Valley.

Still, the champions looked better than most people she'd seen so far. Most of them were dressed in evening suits. The exception was a taller, muscular bald man. His arms were thick like her tights. She would have guessed him descendant from a giant if she didn't know they were just legends. One of his eyes was missing and he had a thick scar from his chin to his head. He was from the Marshes, and it seemed they were unaware that beauty was a thing in this competition. Or else they had sent him to win.

Every time a champion was introduced, there was applause and cheers coming from one corner or the other. They had supporters, probably people from their region. At least Zora had Loretta. If she was there. It was hard to see.

Looking at everyone side-by-side, she realized that Griffin was the shortest champion. Second shortest, if she counted herself. She hadn't noticed that he wasn't tall. But then, being the prince and all, it probably didn't bother him.

She thought the man in gold was going to introduce him, but instead, he moved back to Zora.

"And here, for the first time in the Royal Games, we have a champion from the Dark Valley. I present to you: Zora."

She waved. At least some people applauded. Some even cheered here and there. The loudest cheer came from the band and the artists, who sat on a corner. Zora smiled and waved.

The man then walked to the other edge. "And now, representing the crown, standing here with the champions to remind us that we are all equal, Prince Griffin."

The crowd erupted in cheers and applause. He had the most supporters by far, plus everyone probably felt they had to clap out of respect, considering who he was.

"It's an honor." His voice was surprisingly loud and clear, and he didn't need the cone. "This year, we'll fight for the legendary Blood Cup. It's a privilege seldom bestowed upon us. But it also means it will be much harder than any Royal Games. Those who choose to continue must know that you may lose your life, you may lose your limbs, you may be scarred forever."

He looked at her while he said this.

"It is no dishonor to quit," he continued. Goodness, he really wanted her out. At least he moved his eyes away from her. "But if you put your blood in our chalice, you're committing to certain rules. You guarantee you are the champion chosen by your region. Lies and deceit will be punished by death."

Zora kept her face neutral, almost bored. Death? If they caught her she'd be dead? But how would they catch her? Perhaps Griffin was bluffing. He had glanced at her while saying this.

Then the man in gold started talking on his cone. "There's more. The Blood Cup requires a sacrifice. If you win all the tasks, you'll still have to face and kill a lion, using only a shield, a sword, and a lance."

Zora glanced at the poor animal and felt horrified. "No!" Her scream came out before she realized she should have been quiet.

"You're free to quit," Griffin said, not as loud as he'd been speaking before.

"Excuse me?" The man in gold said in his cone. "Did I hear a no?" He walked to her. "What's the problem?" He asked more in curiosity or if it was something entertaining than as if reproaching her, but she still felt singled out.

"The lion didn't do anything," she said in a small voice, hoping nobody would hear her.

"Do you want to hear what she said?" The man said in the cone. Great.

The arena yelled, "Yes."

The man then put the cone in front of his mouth, and mimicked her voice: "The lion didn't do anything."

There was silence for a moment, then the man started laughing, and the crowd erupted in laughter.

She felt blood rising to her face. She'd never been ridiculed like that in her entire life and all she could do was stare at the ground. No, that was wrong. She looked up and faced the man. "I'm worried about the lion. What's so funny about that?"

The man looked at her. "You're saying that, if you were to face that beast, you'd be afraid—for the lion?"

She shrugged. "He didn't choose to be here." Why wasn't anyone listening to her?

The man was about to say something, but it was Griffin who spoke, loud and clear, to the entire arena. "A sacrifice is necessary for the Blood Cup. This is no normal competition. But if anyone feels uncomfortable with the rules," he looked at her, "there's no dishonor in stepping out. Would anyone like to quit?"

There was only silence. Even the murmurs in the audience had quieted down. Zora rolled her eyes, knowing well that Griffin was hoping she would be out of the competition. The thing is, leaving didn't change the fact that they wanted to kill a lion. Perhaps she could find a way to change that rule. But quitting wasn't it.

"Well, then," the man in gold said. "It's time for you all to commit to the Blood Cup."

He gave each champion a dagger. Griffin cut the palm of his hand and dripped some blood in a small golden chalice that the man carried. All the champions did it in their turn. Zora wondered if the dagger had been properly cleaned. Years of watching her parents had taught her to take infections seriously. Then she decided she'd wash her hand well afterwards, and plus this dagger had probably been kept for years without use. She used the tip to pierce the skin on her thumb, then squeezed it until a red drop came out of it and fell to join the others. She wasn't going to risk hurting her hand for a silly drop of blood.

This was it. She was in the Royal Games. Risking death, but she was there. In theory, it sounded quite dangerous and reckless, except that she'd risked death every single day of her life. At least this time she had the chance to make a difference. That cup was going to be hers. And on top of all that, it would be the best revenge against what Griffin had done to her tonight. And against Seth.

When she got to her room, she found a note:

Library. 8 o'clock.

So the games were about to begin.

6

POETRY & ART

Zora had to stifle a yawn as she walked into the library. Funny place. This time she wouldn't walk into rooms with only one exit.

Larzen himself was there, sitting on a chair, and got up when he saw her.

"Hey." Zora looked around. "We're gonna check books?" The idea was exciting.

"Maybe. But I just said library because you'd know where it is."

"Right. Cause I spent hours here last night. Do you know who did it?"

Larzen shrugged, as they walked to a door outside the castle. "No idea."

He'd said it as if it had been a real question, and she just wanted to give him the answer. "Your brother. He wants me out of the competition."

Larzen snorted. "Griffin? He does want you out, but I doubt he would lock you in a room. It wouldn't be..." He rolled his eyes. "Honorable. And that's one thing he prizes above all else."

"No, no. I'm sure it was him." She then explained exactly what had happened.

"It was not my brother," Larzen insisted.

"You don't believe me?"

"I'm pretty sure you met him, he showed you the right room for the information you wanted, then someone closed the door. No necessary correlation between Griffin and whoever did that. It might have been by mistake. People don't go to the library often anymore."

"Which is a pity. Regardless. I *know* it was Griffin."

"Well, I know it wasn't."

Annoying. But then, what did she expect from Prince Larzen? He wouldn't go against his own brother. Which was a problem, if Griffin wanted to do everything he could to get her out of the competition.

They were walking away from the castle and came to an orchard with grapevines, some flowers, a few trees, and cute stone paths leading to some stone benches.

The prince had a mischievous twinkle in his eyes. "Want to guess why we're here?"

"I'm hoping you'll tell me about the games."

He pinched her cheek. "So adorable. I will. But these are the courting games."

She had no idea they would get started on those games that early, but she had to keep her promise. "What do you want me to do?"

"There's a gentleman who tends to sit at that bench there, by the apple tree. He'll be here... I don't know. In some time. All I want you to do is sit on that bench. If he complains and says you should move, you don't move."

Zora frowned. "What's that supposed to accomplish?"

"See that beautiful tree?" Larzen pointed at it.

"Yeah."

"It might be big, now, but it used to be just a seed. A tiny seed. You plant the seeds first. Get the fruit later."

"And not moving from the bench will plant some love seeds?"

He laughed. His laughter was just like Griffin's. "You don't start by planting love, dear. You plant intrigue."

She wasn't going to argue with crazy. "Fine. But don't blame me when no tree grows. And who is he, by the way?"

"You can't know, right? Or the game will look rigged. Don't show interest. And please, don't second-guess yourself, wondering if it's working, what he's thinking. It kills the seeds."

She wasn't going to wonder any of that. She was wondering if Larzen was crazy.

"Oh," he added, and pulled a small book from his pocket. "You'll be reading this. If he asks you about the poems, you can discuss them. But focus more on the book than on him."

Zora shrugged, but did what the prince told her. Maybe it was a game, but she was pretty certain these weren't the right moves. But then, what did she know about it?

She sat and opened the book. Poetry. Neat. There was just one poetry book in the Dark Valley, and she had read it so many times that reading was no longer necessary. As she read some poems, her stomach started to churn. Love poems. Ugh. The author was some dude named Develson Wilson, and most poems were complex love declarations. Zora got the feeling that they weren't all to the same girl, though. Then some of the poems were about the agony of loving someone. That, she could understand.

Somebody should write poems about the stupidity of loving someone who didn't deserve to be loved. Or the satisfaction of taking their place in a competition. Zora exhaled. So far she hadn't been caught. Each second that passed meant her chances of staying were higher.

A lot of time passed and nobody came. She wanted to strangle the author of the book for the lies he was writing. Nobody could possibly love that much, right? She decided to lie down on the bench.

Somebody cleared their throat.

Zora sat up and saw a young man with dark hair and hazel eyes. His face was quite nice, with a well-formed jaw, full lips, and lashes that would make any girl die with envy. And she looked away. Pretty sure that noticing the guy's hotness was not part of Larzen's plan. Perhaps the intriguing thing would be anyone ignoring him.

But she could be polite. Zora smiled. "Hi. Did you want anything?"

"That's my bench you're sitting on."

Zora looked around. "I see no name here. Or sign. And there are other benches over there."

"In the sun."

"Sun is nice. Better than shadows."

"Could you move?"

Oh, so much entitlement! "No. I got here first. But there's room for two."

The guy stared at her for seconds and seconds, still standing, then noticed her book. "Where did you get this?"

"The library. You know, the place where they have books?" All right. Zora was enjoying this.

He frowned. "And why did you choose this?"

Shit, shit, shit. She had to come up with an explanation

fast. "I didn't choose it. It was on a table and I took it. Then I was surprised at learning that men can write words about love."

"That's ridiculous. If men didn't love, most love stories wouldn't exist."

Zora shrugged. "I guess." She decided to lie down again.

"So you're not going to move?"

"I can sit up and we can share the bench."

He didn't say anything. After long moments, he asked, "Can you really slay a lion?"

That made her sit. He must have seen her in the arena. Why were they misunderstanding her so much? "I'd rather not."

"So you're not here to win."

"I'd rather win without killing an innocent creature, but I will if I have to."

His hazel eyes sparkled. "That innocent creature would devour you if given the chance."

"It's its nature."

He tilted his head. "What about the shadow creatures in the Dark Valley? Isn't it their nature to kill, too?"

She frowned. Where was he getting at? "Well, they aren't really alive. If we hit them enough, they disappear. Who knows, they might go back to living in peace in whatever realm they're from. So it's different."

"I guess." He looked away, then back at her. "Which of these poems is your favorite?"

Zora was surprised. "You've read this? You like poetry, too?"

"Love and art. That's all life is about. The rest is fluff. And yeah, I read it."

"Which is *your* favorite?"

71

"I asked first."

She decided to be honest. "I like the one where he compares love to poison, killing you slowly and causing agonizing pain. It's the most realistic."

He raised his eyebrows. "Glad you like it. I'll take your offer."

"What?"

"Move. We're sharing this bench." He sat down and looked at her. "You're beautiful."

That was fast. Or weird.

"But these words are empty," he added. "Beautiful are the birds in the field, the sky in the morning, the flowers we step on. Beauty is unreachable. And yet superficial. And yet I— I feel there's more beauty. Beauty inside. And that's what I mean to find. If only you let me try."

Zora exhaled. "Let me in." At least it wasn't one of those nausea-inducing eternal love declarations. It wasn't that good, either, but whatever. She shook the book. "Page thirty-four. That's your favorite?"

He tilted his head. "Maybe."

His eyes were fixed on her and she felt awkward. Zora got up. "You know what? You can have the bench. I have to train. But it was nice meeting you. Can I have your name?"

He laughed. That laugh... It couldn't be. Unless everyone in the castle had the same laugh. Maybe.

He said, "Names are superficial, aren't they?"

"It's how you know who is who."

He smirked. "My name won't tell you who I am. Your name won't tell me who you are."

Right. "Nice seeing you, then." Zora turned around and walked away. Awkward. At least Larzen hadn't asked her to flirt or anything.

Now, she certainly hoped the guy from the orchard wasn't who she was thinking. If it was, she'd have disgraced herself with two-thirds of the existing royal family. That wasn't good.

Hopefully she'd done her part well with the one third who still wasn't against her.

As she walked back to her room, somebody pulled her hand. Larzen stood behind a huge statue in the hallway.

"I have good news and bad news for you," he said.

"Bad news first, or they'll spoil the good news. Did you see me in the orchard?"

"Maybe. But remember not to second-guess yourself." He tapped her nose with his finger.

"Was he... your brother?" Zora asked.

"If you didn't figure it out, I'm not going to tell you. Do you want the news or not?"

"Yes."

He had a sort of scarf in his hand. "I'll have to blindfold you. Secret passages."

That required a lot of trust, but she had no choice. Plus she still had her sword Butterfly on her back and figured she could hold her own. Zora turned around. "Go ahead."

He wrapped the cloth around her head. Zora wanted to lift it and peak, but he held her hands as they descended stairs and more stairs. It smelled humid and moldy, and she assumed she was in some kind of cellar or basement.

When Larzen stopped, he said, "Ta-da!" and pulled her blindfold.

Zora was in the dungeons, in front of a cell with iron bars. In it, on a corner, sleeping, was Seth. Seth, the guy she had left behind in the Dark Valley, the guy whose chance at coming to the castle she had stolen. The guy who should have been back in that valley. But instead, he was here. Zora froze.

Larzen took her chin. "I'm going to say only once. Do. Not. Lie. To me. Ever again."

"But..."

"Shush. If you insist on your little lie, I'm going to wake him up and we'll set up a royal court. Let's see how well you do when it's your word against his and mine. Want to try?"

"No."

He let go of her. "Good. Now I'm serious. Do. Not. Lie. I can't help you if there's no trust between us. You are so, so very lucky he was brought to me. Do you know who he should have been brought to?"

Zora had a guess. "Griffin."

"And do you want to guess who he would believe?"

She looked down. "I'm sorry."

"Well, great reason to be sorry. If it wasn't for me, sometime tomorrow we'd be separating your head from your body. How would you like that?"

She had no answer.

"I'm going to be clear." Larzen was pointing a finger at her. "Lie to me again, and I'll make sure this guy gets out and tells his story. Same thing if you get funny ideas and stop playing my game. Is that understood?"

"Yes." She glanced at Seth. He didn't look hurt, but still. She felt guilty that he was imprisoned. "Will he be all right?"

"As all right as someone in a cell can be."

Zora felt bad, but then she remembered what Seth had said and done, and thought it was deserved. Seeing his face reminded her of all the fake promises, false kisses, the way he kept pushing her, insisting. And he shouldn't have followed her. He could have caused her death. Perhaps she shouldn't pity him. Seth in Gravel city was a constant threat to her. "Why is he asleep? What's gonna happen when he wakes up?"

"I didn't want you two talking. Now, these are my cells. Handy, right? I can make sure whatever he says stays here. If you help me. And if you stop lying."

"I will help you, for sure."

"Great." Larzen raised an eyebrow as he stared at her. "Tell me. Is it true you stole his letter and rod in the middle of the night? Is it true you didn't even *enter* the competition to represent your valley?"

Zora sighed. "It's true."

His eyes narrowed. "Why then... why are you here?"

She decided to be honest. "Petty revenge. He was my boyfriend. Or I thought so. But he was a liar and a cheater and didn't plan to come back. So..." It was hard to say it because it sounded awful, but strangely, she didn't feel any shame or regret. "I took his place."

Larzen stared at her for a moment, then laughed. "Scorned women. Dangerous thing."

"It's not that I was scorned. It's the lies. Had he been honest..." Just the memory brought a bitter taste to her mouth.

"Lies. Aren't they awful? You should have told me what was happening."

She realized her life depended on Larzen. "Thank you. Thank you so much. For forgiving me."

He waved a hand. "You'll have tons of opportunities to show me your thankfulness."

Zora wanted to change the subject. "And what is the good news?"

Larzen smiled. "I know what's going to be in the first challenge. And you're right. Griffin really wants you out."

THESE FIELDS WERE SO FAR from the castle that nobody should see them—hopefully. Griffin still wondered what he was doing, still regretted some of his decisions. Yet here he was galloping side by side with Alegra, her loose dress flowing about her. Sometimes he thought she enjoyed the thrill of maybe getting caught. For Griffin, it gave him headaches. And yet he wasn't strong enough to say no. The right thing would be for them to wait until it was clear that there was nothing between her and Kiran. And yet he wasn't waiting.

There was something else. He wasn't being completely honest with the princess. He'd come today to tell her. Tell her the secret almost nobody knew, the secret that could cost him his life. The issue was that he'd have to trust her, and a small part of him wasn't ready to do that. On the other hand, how could he demand her to make a choice, to give up on what would be a beneficial marriage, if she didn't yet know what Griffin was? He needed her full commitment in order to trust her, and yet, it was unfair to demand it without telling her everything. It was a dilemma to which he had no answer. Perhaps the field and the air would help him find a solution.

"Griffin!" Alegra had her horse right beside his. "Why do you ask me to spend time with you, when your mind is miles and miles away?" Her tone was playful.

She was right. "I'm sorry."

Her gaze then became piercing and serious. "You're troubled."

If anything, Alegra was always insightful, as if she could look at his soul. And it seemed that, despite everything, she liked it. And maybe that was the answer. If she loved him, she'd want him regardless. She wasn't losing anything by not marrying his brother.

Griffin smiled. "Never any trouble when I'm with you."

She laughed. "Liar. Is it the cup?"

That, too. Maybe. A little. It was his one chance to find his way out. It was perhaps the reason he hadn't yet told Alegra anything. Perhaps he wouldn't have to. He knew he could win. "No, it's fine. I'm confident about it."

"Wouldn't it be nicer to let one of your subjects win?"

He didn't want to tell her how badly he wanted the cup, so he said, "There's value in competing against them. It elevates the competition for all the participants."

"But if you win, it proves that you're better than them. Is that what you're after?"

"Monarchy is old and entrenched in our way of thinking. I don't think I need to do anything to establish my superiority. I'm not even sure of that."

She narrowed her eyes. "Quite humble, for someone who believes he'll win."

"Everything starts with belief, right? And it's just a competition to entertain visitors. Doesn't prove anything."

"And..." She paused. "Is it true you're worried about the Dark Valley girl?"

Strange that she was bringing this up. "Not really. She'll be out in this challenge. Then we can move to more dangerous stuff."

"Why do you want her out? Is it because of what happened in the Oak Tavern?" She laughed.

"Strangely, no. I forgot about that, and maybe I'm not that upset. It led me to a cold bath that ended up not being so terrible." He gave her a pointed look.

Her cheeks turned pink and she said, "We could swim in a lake today."

"I'd rather be careful."

Alegra scrunched her face. "Sometimes you're so boring."

"Maybe you like boring."

She laughed, then got serious. "You still haven't answered, though."

"What?"

"What's your issue with the girl?"

His mind had been somewhere else, perhaps pondering the risks of going for a swim. Griffin shrugged. "She's too pretty."

Alegra froze. Her eyes flashed something like fury for a second.

"What?" Griffin shuddered. "Don't tell me you're jealous. There are thousands of pretty girls in the world. None of them half as lovely as you. And I'm thinking about my subjects. They wouldn't want to see her getting hurt."

She glared at him. "I'm not jealous. She's a poor peasant from the worst place in the kingdom. Nobody would even look at her."

"I don't think so. She could find a good husband. You know I want to have better relations with the Dark Valley."

Alegra sighed. "You mean well, Griffin. Your heart is good, and that's what I like about you. But I hope you didn't tell her she had any odds of getting married. She's got nothing to offer. She's neither rich nor a noble."

Griffin shrugged. "I don't know. Some younger brothers don't have pressure for marriage. Sometimes all they want is someone to embrace after their day is done."

Alegra rolled her eyes. "You mean someone to bang. You might have a point."

"What? No. Someone to love. A companion, a friend, and yes, sure, a lover, too. You say it as if there was something wrong with it. Are you going to say it means a woman is *serving a man*?" He shuddered remembering it.

She laughed. "Absolutely not. If anything, I think you're serving me."

Griffin shook his head.

Alegra continued laughing. "Nothing to be ashamed of. You do it pretty well."

Griffin just sighed.

She then got serious and continued, "But you're forgetting a key point. Younger brothers are the ones who most need to find good matches, Griffin."

He stopped. "Is that what you think I'm doing with you? Because I would still marry you, and *serve you,* if that's how you like to put it, if you were not a princess, if you were poor. I hope you know that."

She shrugged. "No doubt you believe that. But we wouldn't even have met if I hadn't come here representing my kingdom, so maybe you need to get some reality check in that empty head of yours."

Sometimes Alegra's teasing went overboard. And she was wrong. "Well, the Dark Valley girl will meet people, so I don't see why not. She'll be happy, I'll be happy, and I won't offend the Dark Valley."

Alegra narrowed her eyes, as if trying to find out something. "Why do you care about that valley?"

Dark magic. He had to learn everything he could about dark magic. And maybe they had the answer to his problem. But Griffin just shrugged. "They're part of the kingdom, too. And if it weren't for them, shadow creatures would overrun us. It's time we acknowledge that."

"Wasn't it their own ancestor's fault that those creatures were let loose in the first place?"

"That's what the books say. Who knows? It's been so long.

Either way, they're paying their dues and they're part of the kingdom, too."

She approached her horse and pinched his cheek. "So fair and idealistic."

He closed his eyes. "You're making fun of me?"

"On the contrary. I think it's quite hot." She looked ahead. "Is that a lake?"

"Yes, but—"

She had galloped ahead of him and was descending from the horse. He meant to say they weren't going to stop there.

When he caught up, she was already tying her mount and unlacing her dress, smiling at him. "I'm going for a swim. You can watch or you can come. Your choice."

"This lake has a muddy bottom."

"I don't mind mud." Her dress fell down and she picked it up. Now she was just in her undergarments. "But don't worry. I'll make sure my clothes don't get wet this time."

This was a terrible, reckless idea. Griffin dismounted and tied his horse. Alegra was running towards the water and he was impressed with the speed she had undressed. He sighed and sat on a rock. He could control anger, he could control darkness, he could control other stuff, too. And yet he wondered what it would be like to feel the soft, dark mud from the banks against his skin. But getting caught could get them killed.

Then, maybe not. If it was true that there was nothing between Alegra and Kiran, that they hadn't even kissed, and that their betrothal more and more was unlikely to happen, what was the problem? His mind told him that he should wait. Wait until everything was confirmed. Wait until he knew for sure he wasn't betraying his brother. And yet that dark, sticky mud was calling to him.

7

THE FIRST CHALLENGE

It was night when all the competitors entered the arena. Larzen's tip had given Zora time to make a potion for better night vision. They didn't use those much in the Dark Valley, considering everything was always lit, but she was glad she knew it. Her bedroom had now a potion-making table, and thankfully Loretta didn't mind it. And just to be safe, she had drunk a potion for precision and speed, too.

Larzen hadn't told her all the details of the competition, only that a lot of it would be in the dark. Zora couldn't quite see the point of doing it without light. Wasn't it supposed to be entertaining? What would audiences see? But hey, it wasn't her call. Stupid Griffin probably thought she would freak out in the dark. Didn't he remember she'd been locked in a dark room in a library for a long time? Unless he had no idea the lamp had gone out. At least her experience had been useful.

Despite being prepared and telling herself that she had great odds, her heart was beating fast. What if the other champions were faster? What if they also knew it would be in the dark and had drunk potions too? No, Larzen had said that potion-making was a rare activity in the kingdom. She didn't feel like she was cheating. Wasn't the competition about testing their minds, too?

Stavos arranged them in a line. Griffin was first, Zora was second. She wondered if the order was that just so that he would stand beside someone shorter than him. That was a mean thought. They entered through a side door this time, and stood again at a semi-circle, but in a corner. There were poles with a line and thick burlap hanging from it, so that it blocked the middle of the arena from their view. It was still unfair that Griffin knew details about the competition when they didn't. But then, according to Larzen, he only knew broad strokes, just like her.

Before the champions were announced, Griffin whispered to her, "Yell for help if you need."

"Shouldn't the other champions be told that, too?"

Griffin had a grimace. "I think they know."

"Well, thanks so much for the reminder, then." She laced her words in sarcasm.

"No problem." Griffin gave her a polite nod, as if she had really been thanking him.

All right. He thought she was an idiot. Charming. But she had to forget that.

Zora took a deep breath. She knew that the secret to fighting well was to be both alert and calm. Nerves could blind you. Whatever was behind those burlaps, she would face it as if she were facing a dark creature attack back home.

She wished she weren't standing by Griffin, though. Yes, it was stupid of him to underestimate her, he was the dumber of them both, and yet still he unsettled her. Perhaps it was just the knowledge that he wanted her out of the competition and would do anything he could to achieve that, including tailoring the challenges to her weaknesses. Ha. Weaknesses. Again he underestimated her. All he was doing was making her want that cup more than ever just to spite him.

A happy thought came to her mind, then. At least her hate for Griffin had made her stop thinking about Seth and all he'd done. Perhaps the heart had a special place for one hated person, just like it had a special place for love, although she swore to leave that empty or fill it with love for humanity, for her valley.

The burlaps were brought down. There were low fences in what looked like some kind of labyrinth. The lights in the audience were turned off, so that all they could see were the lamps illuminating the middle field. It was strange to be surrounded by that invisible audience immersed in darkness. Zora could feel their energy, their hum, hear them, and yet, she couldn't see them.

The presenter was wearing bright purple this time. He gave each competitor a bag made of some kind of net.

"Pay attention, champions! Once we open the field, you'll find tons of black balls. The one who catches the most is the winner. The three with the least balls will be eliminated. But watch out. You can only move in the dark. When the lights are on, you have to stop. There will be penalties for players who don't stop. You can only move when lights are off."

Interesting. But in theory, they could see things when the lights were off, if the eyes adjusted to the dark. Especially Zora's eyes, with her potion. But then when they turned on the lights it would mess it up. Unless... She closed her left eye, waiting for the signal. All at once, the lanterns were covered. Zora closed her right eye and opened her left. It wasn't that bad, she could see everything in tones of grey. She noticed that they were people on the edges throwing new balls so that the existing balls would move. She ran fast, ignoring the closest balls because she wanted some distance from the other champions. Having them all in the dark would be a good opportunity for some unsavory actions. It was forbidden and could get a champion kicked out, but she didn't doubt anything. Plus, she wanted more room for herself.

When the lights went on again, she hadn't caught a single ball but was far from the other competitors. She made sure to close her left eye so that it would still be adjusted to the dark. When it got dark again, she closed her right eye and picked balls as fast as she could. They weren't that easy to see, being black over dark ground, but she could still spot them. She didn't know how well her competitors were doing.

When the light went on again, the champions were more spread out and there were fewer balls on the field. Zora thought she was doing well and took the next turn to give herself more space from the competitors instead of picking balls. Later she noticed that other champions were following her strategy, but she was far and with tons of balls for herself. She even wondered if she should take it easy so as not to bring any suspicion, but then decided that she'd rather win with a large difference if she could. That would teach Griffin not to try to get her eliminated.

The competition ended with a loud bell. They all walked to the front and the man in purple counted their balls. Zora had twenty-four. Griffin himself had come close to her, with twenty-two. The third competitor had sixteen. The huge scarred guy from the Marshes had fourteen. A bunch of champions had ten and eleven. Finally, one champion had eight, and two had nine balls. So close! They were the ones who were eliminated. The presenter invited the audience to cheer on their bravery and skill. Poor champions, never really had a chance to prove any bravery. Either way, some had to be eliminated.

Zora was ecstatic when she stepped forward and got cheers for having won that challenge. Yes, yes! Take that, Seth. Take that, Griffin. She was competent and she was there to win. Her eyes crossed Griffin's. He was rather examining her, as if thoughtful. Hopefully reconsidering his first dumb impressions. She smirked. He nodded politely. Zora looked away. Somehow she preferred his evil eye.

As the competition finished, Zora had a second race to attend. There would be a ball in an hour. Of course, the champions could arrive a little late, but not too much. Lovely and wonderful for the men who only had to take a bath and change. She wasn't even that sure about the bath. Lovely for the women who had come to the arena half ready, at least with hair and make-up. For all that Griffin said he wanted Zora to meet people, he hadn't considered that she needed time to get ready for a ball. Well, duh. He was a guy and probably thought women were naturally born with makeup and hair done.

Thankfully, Larzen was helping her, with two attendants who were fast at work. The dress he had chosen for her had a color like golden yellow on top, then got darker and darker until it looked like a starry sky in the bottom. It was almost like a message telling people that she could deal with the night. The dress was a bit extravagant for Zora's taste, but then, she didn't know that much about court fashion. Or rather, she didn't know anything about it. Without Larzen's help, she would have nothing to wear. The champions did get a small stipend, but the issue would be that she didn't even have any idea where to buy dresses, nevermind the time to take care of that. Having allies was good.

Zora was also happy for having Loretta. Going to her first

ball with a friend made it slightly less scary, and hopefully would make it a lot more fun. Loretta had a gorgeous burgundy dress, bringing out her dark hair. When they reached the ballroom, it had a lot of people already. A master-of-ceremony took their names, but didn't announce them as they came in. Still, many people looked at Zora. They probably had seen her in the arena. It felt odd to have random people recognizing her. She also felt a little self-conscious because other women's dresses weren't as extravagant as hers. It was as if Larzen had dressed her to draw even more eyes. Well, if that was the game she had to play, she'd play it.

Loretta had sharp eyes on the people. "So you don't recommend any of the champions?"

"I don't know them."

Her friend then looked down and put a hand over her forehead, as if willing to hide. "I can't believe this."

"What?"

"Ephemerus. He has a shop in a city close by. He's my business rival."

Zora wanted to ask who it was, but then thought that pointing would be too obvious. "You probably won't even talk."

Loretta grimaced as a very good-looking young man with dark, curly hair and brown skin approached them.

"Lady Loretta," he said. "What a pleasant surprise. Would you give me the pleasure of the next dance?"

"Sure," Loretta said with a smile that didn't reach her eyes. She then turned to Zora. "I'll be right back."

They moved to the center of the ballroom. A small band with strings and percussion played in a corner, but it wasn't as loud as it had been in the arena. Maybe the idea was that people could talk over their sound.

Zora felt awkward to be alone, without a single person

she knew. Even the princes were not there. Not that she thought Larzen would be hanging out with her. She should perhaps get to know some of the champions. On a table by a corner, alone, she found the huge competitor from the Marshes, who had a scar in place of an eye, and felt bad that people weren't socializing with him, maybe because of his looks. Zora didn't like that. In the valley, scars were common, and only meant that the person had fought and survived.

She approached his table and pulled a chair. "Can I sit?"

The man shrugged and looked away. "It's empty."

She knew that attitude, as she'd seen in some of her students. He was pushing people away so that it didn't seem that anyone was rejecting him, but rather that it was his choice. In fact, he could wear an eye patch or something, but probably wanted to keep the menacing appearance.

Then he added, "And I don't do the matchmaking thing. I have someone."

Zora smiled as she sat. "That's great. I'm not into match-making either. Not that I have anyone. What's your name?"

"You didn't hear it?"

"Hear, yeah, catch, no. But I did catch that you're from the Marshes. Or am I confused?"

"Marshes, yeah. I'm Mauro. And you're Zora, from the Dark Valley."

"In person." She smiled.

"Congratulations on the win." He sounded sincere.

"Thanks. You did well yourself." He'd caught some sixteen balls.

"I guess." He nodded and was thoughtful. "In your valley, is it true that creatures will spawn even in small spaces?"

"It is."

"What do you do with your shoes when you're not wearing them?"

That was actually a good question. "We flatten them." She spread her hands on the table, as if flattening a boot. "They're usually made of flexible material."

"What about when you sleep? Under your blankets?"

"No blankets or sheets."

Mauro was surprised. "Don't you get cold?"

"We dress warm. Sometimes light fires."

"But you can't have chimneys, can you?"

The guy was smart. That was something she would need to keep in mind. Strong like that, one would think he was all brawn and no brains, but it didn't seem to be the case. But she didn't mind answering him. "We light fires on the outside. Our houses are made with stone or other materials that don't catch fire."

"Lots of work."

That was true. "We're used to it. What about the Marshes? What's life like there?"

"Normal. My family raises cattle. There's fishing in the rivers."

"Doesn't it, like, get all flooded some times of the year?"

"It does. We use more boats, then." He stared at her with his one functioning eye. "Look, I see you're being nice and all, but it could be my life against yours in the arena. And I know which one I'm choosing."

"You think I'm trying to get your help?"

He shook his head. "I'm just explaining why I'm being reserved. And I don't want to talk about the competition. Or try to form alliances just to be stabbed in the back later or something."

Zora shrugged. "At least you take me seriously as a competitor. Can't say the same of everyone."

"Their problem. Underestimating your adversaries is the quickest path to defeat."

"I don't think they see me as an adversary, even after today."

Mauro thought for a moment. "Well, to be fair, not all champions are here to win. Some came here for... networking opportunities, if you get my gist. So it's not a completely unfounded assumption. Wrong, of course."

Maybe. In the case of Griffin, he was well aware that she hadn't come just for networking opportunities and still he underestimated her. She looked at Mauro. "How do you know I'm an adversary?"

"Assumptions are the counsel of the dumb."

"Indeed." She had a cup with red juice and lifted it. "Cheers."

He raised his own cup, which seemed to have water. At least Zora had someone to talk to while her friend danced. Loretta didn't look very happy. Hopefully she'd find better partners soon.

The music stopped.

"Please stand up for the royal family," the master of ceremony said.

Zora stood up and saw Griffin, in an elegant black suit, Larzen, in bright blue, which still somehow looked good on him, matching his eyes, and the person she feared, wearing beige and gold witch contrasted with his hair and sort of matched his hazel eyes. It was King Kiran, of course, but it was also the guy in the orchard. Zora wished she could dig a hole and hide. But then, if Larzen's game was for her to make a fool of herself to the king, so be it. It wasn't as if she was in a position to say no to whatever schemes he had.

A few minutes later, Loretta came back. She had a big smile and seemed genuinely happy to meet Mauro, asking him about his region.

When he got up to get a drink, Loretta whispered to Zora, "Aren't they beautiful? They look better in person than in paintings."

"You mean the princes and the king?"

"Of course." Loretta had a quiet laugh. "Who do you think is the best looking?"

Griffin. The word popped in her head for some weird reason. Zora shuddered. It made no sense. Kiran and Larzen were better looking. "Larzen," she said. At least he was her ally.

"His eyes are something else. But I still prefer King Kiran."

"Well, it's not like we're gonna have to choose." Zora laughed. Then she noticed Ephemerus approaching. "Your friend, or rival, is coming."

"That's so annoying."

"Can't you say no to a dance?"

Loretta rolled her eyes. "It's considered rude, especially if you already know the person."

"I see."

Hopefully he wouldn't want to dance again with her friend. But he did. Loretta was gone.

Zora was wondering if she should get up or something, when Larzen approached her.

He raised an eyebrow. "Sitting on a corner, dejected, after tonight's victory?"

"I'm not dejected."

He extended his hand. "Come, then. Let's dance."

For real? A prince was inviting her to dance? "Am I allowed to dance with your highness?"

Larzen snorted. "There's no law against it. And it's all part of the game."

Zora got up and followed him to the center of the room. She tried to follow his movements, careful not to step on his feet or fall. When she was sure there was nobody close to them, she said, "He's the king."

Larzen shrugged. "So?"

"Well. My behavior wasn't what he would expect—"

"And that's why it works." He pinched her nose.

"You don't actually expect him to..." She wasn't even sure what to say. Get interested in her? She looked down. "I don't know."

"Try not to worry about it. I'm not asking you to flirt with him, am I?"

She shook her head.

He smiled. "Perfect. Understand what we're doing here. We're setting up the bait. Let him bite. Want to know why I'm dancing with you?"

"Because I look gorgeous with the dress you picked?" She laughed. "No. To talk, right?"

"Maybe. Now think. What happens once people see you dancing with me?"

Zora didn't really want to think about that. "Hum. They'll think we know each other. Or maybe that you..." Again she didn't want to voice her thoughts and looked down.

"So shy. You need to finish your sentences, miss. What were you saying?"

"Some people might think you're interested in me."

"Perfect. So what happens next?"

Zora had no clue. "I don't know."

"You know what happens when someone from the royal family starts using a specific tailor?"

They didn't have that job in the Dark Valley, but she could guess. "The tailor gets famous."

"Exactly. People will want to know what is special about him. And that's what happens to you now."

"That's kind of embarrassing."

"No, no, Zora. If you want to play the game, you can't be embarrassed. You can't think that you're not worthy of a prince. Or a king."

Zora wondered if he was right in the head, but decided not to argue. She could hide her emotions, so she smiled. "You're absolutely right."

She was definitely sure Kiran would never be interested in her, but if pretending to believe it made his brother happy, so be it. For all she knew, it could be some kind of cruel prank, but she didn't care as long as she got tips for the competition and he took care of Seth.

Larzen smiled. "And you're right that you do look gorgeous in this dress. Do you find yourself beautiful?"

Seth and his friend's talk came to her mind, but she tried to forget it. "I'm usually happy with the way I look." True. Especially now that she didn't care what people would think about her.

"You need to be a little happier. Did you know that most women think they're uglier than they actually are?"

Zora laughed. "I see young teens thinking that. I tell them all that they're beautiful. But it's the same with men, isn't it?"

"Maybe. But they're under the impression that their personality makes up for the lack of good looks. Not me. I think I'm quite blessed in terms of appearance."

"It's unfair. Not only you're a prince, you're handsome."

He smiled as if satisfied with a compliment. It wasn't a compliment, just the truth.

He said, "Well, life is not fair. Now onto our game. If people ask you to dance, accept. Don't be upset if only a few men approach you. Not only you're a champion, you're dancing with me. It's intimidating."

"Wasn't it going to make me famous like a tailor?"

"Yes. But only for those who believe they can afford it, right?"

"This is all new to me so I'll trust you on that."

"That's a smart move." He pinched her nose again.

The song ended, then he bowed and moved away. Zora went back to her seat.

Loretta and Mauro were there. Mauro seemed bored. Loretta's jaw was dropped. "The prince. You danced with the prince," she whispered.

"Because I'm a champion. He's... just being polite."

She chuckled. "If people hear about it, next time all regions are going to send girls."

"As long as they're here to win, that's good. Speaking of which, which champion is from the Gold Port?"

"Klaus. He's blond with dark tan skin."

"He was standing by me when we were introduced."

"Yes. He comes from a family of poor fishermen. I wish him luck."

"You're supporting him, right?"

"You two. Both of you. He's from my region. You're a woman like me. The third champion I support is Mauro." She turned to him.

He laughed. "No need to lie."

"It's true," Loretta protested. "You're our friend."

That was funny. Zora herself was thinking of Mauro as just

an acquaintance. But it actually felt good to feel that she had one more friend.

"Thank you," he said, then smiled. "Friends, then."

Zora took her glass and raised it. "To friendship."

They both raised their glasses in a toast.

"What a lovely group of friends," a female voice said. Zora turned. Alegra was there. Her dress was dark blue contrasting with that awesome red hair. She had a sort of unreal beauty.

"Alegra! You're here!" Zora was happy to see her even if she felt plain near her.

"Yes. And who are your friends?"

Zora introduced them and they shook hands. Alegra then took Zora's hands in hers. "You were so amazing tonight. What an inspiration."

"Thank you."

Alegra then added, "And you look so good!"

"You look amazing, too."

Way more than amazing, but she probably knew that already. Or maybe not, if Larzen was right. No, Alegra was someone who was clearly aware of the effect she had on people, with the poise and confidence Zora would never match. But it didn't matter, did it? Zora had to be good at fighting shadow creatures, she didn't have to be drop-dead gorgeous. A part of her wished she could be that pretty, though, as if it would prevent heartbreak.

Alegra sat by her. "Listen, if you ever need a friend, I mean, another friend, as I see you're in great company, don't hesitate to call me. If you ever have any problem, if you ever need an ear, someone to talk to, I'm here."

That was surprising. They barely knew each other. Perhaps people outside the valley were just friendly to strangers, since they didn't grow up knowing everyone around them. "How can I find you?"

"Ask your attendant. They should find me." She squeezed Zora's hand. "Keep being amazing and representing us. Show these men what a woman can do." She glanced at Mauro. "No offense."

"What?" It didn't seem like he'd been hearing them.

Alegra smiled. "Nothing." She turned to Zora. "Good luck."

It was so great to be surrounded by so much support. It even made her forget about Seth in the dungeons. Actually, now that she thought about it, she remembered it, together with an uneasiness in knowing that Larzen had a lot of power over her. But he'd been nice so far. In a way, he was another friend.

Someone stood by her. Kiran, the king. She felt a chill down her spine, but bowed her head. "Your majesty."

8

BEING SEEN

Kiran smirked. "Got better manners now? As tonight's winner, I'd like to present you with a dance."

"Thank you." Zora got up and took his hand.

So arrogant. It was true that he was king, but he could at least ask like a normal person instead of offering the dance as if it were a prize. But he was the king. And accepting the dance was likely part of Larzen's game. No, his game was for her to defy him.

Zora smiled. "Has your majesty ever heard about asking a girl for a dance?"

"Indeed." He smiled back. "So glad I don't have to. So now you figured out who I am?"

"Kind of hard to ignore, when you're announced to everyone."

"So, have you read any more poetry?"

"I need to return that book." That was true, but she wasn't even sure if it had come from the library. "I haven't checked anything else. Busy training."

"It looks like it worked."

"I'm glad it did."

He wrinkled his forehead, as if thoughtful. "It was quite a boring challenge, if I may say. I wonder how you'd fare if it had been more physical."

"I guess we'll have to see."

"Everyone's betting you'll be out in the next challenge, but then, they were betting you'd be out tonight."

Zora smiled. "There's betting? I need to find it and bet on myself."

He laughed. "That's smart. If you're that confident."

"I am." She had to be.

"One day I'd like to discuss poetry with you again. And love, maybe. Would you be interested in that?"

"Maybe." Truth is, she had no clue what to reply and wasn't sure where he was going with it. "As long as nobody convinces me to fall in love, if it's just theory, it's a subject like any other."

"Life is boring when you don't fall in love, don't you think?"

"No. I have other exciting challenges."

"What about making love?"

Zora didn't like his tone or his question, but tried not to show it and just smiled. "If it's not theory, I'm out."

"Fascinating way to live." He shook his head. "I think I'd rather die."

"People have different tastes."

"I suppose you're not sleeping with my brother, then."

Zora stopped, heat coming to her face. "Why would you say that?"

He laughed and put his hands on her shoulders. "So offended. Relax. Larzen's renowned for the games he plays. I was just wondering. I would be careful around him if I were you, that's all."

"I can take care of myself."

"That's good to know." The music stopped. He smiled. "This is it, then. Congratulations on your victory." He squeezed her shoulder.

"Thank you, your majesty."

Zora sat down feeling bothered. Something about his tone had made her uncomfortable, even if the words were not that bad. Well, actually, straight up insinuating she was sleeping with Larzen was pretty gross.

Loretta was all smiles. "Goodness, you danced with the king."

Zora looked down and shrugged. "Because I'm a champion."

"Like I said, you have your privileges!"

"I guess."

Loretta then danced with another merchant. Hopefully it would be someone she would like. Zora observed the multitude in silence. Mauro was also quiet.

The masters of ceremony interrupted the music. "King Kiran has an announcement for us."

Everyone turned to watch. Kiran stood on a small platform. "Dear subjects and esteemed visitors, since the tragic death of my parents, responsibilities have fallen on my shoulders. One of these responsibilities is to produce heirs. It's my duty to get married.I took this duty to heart. Some of you may have heard whispers, and if you heard them, they are true. I know that tonight we're also celebrating our beloved champions in the Blood Cup. Cheers to our lovely Zora."

He pointed at her and smiled. People clapped politely. She wanted to hide under a table, but smiled and waved instead.

When the claps subsided, Kiran continued, "I don't want to outshine anyone but rather add to these celebrations by announcing my betrothal. Alegra, Princess of Linaria, please come forward."

So she was a princess. And what a gorgeous princess. No wonder he had chosen her. Alegra stood by him, looking down as if shy. Kiran took her hand and raised it. "I present to you my future wife, our future queen."

He then kissed her softly on the lips. It was nice to see a couple in love. There was something hopeful and beautiful about it.

But then Zora felt uncomfortable with the talk in the orchard and when she was dancing with Kiran, and regretted being part of whatever games Larzen was planning. Especially when Alegra was so nice. But then, it wasn't as if the king would ignore Alegra for Zora, right? So in theory there had been nothing wrong. Still, she felt bad.

"It's a good alliance," Mauro said, which was good to snap her out of the guilty ride.

"For sure. And she's lovely."

Still, the guilt wouldn't go away, even if technically nothing had happened between her and Kiran and she hadn't flirted with him. All she could do from now on was avoid the king, not that it would be hard, as it wasn't as if they were buddies or anything.

Tired from the competition, she decided to return to her bedroom and turned to Mauro. "I'm going to rest. Enjoy the rest of the party."

He laughed. "Oh, I'll keep having a great time."

Zora chuckled, then left. As she got into the corridor, someone pulled her arm towards the back of a tapestry. It was Larzen.

"Where do you think you are going?" He sounded angry.

"I wanted to rest."

"That's not our deal, darling." There was acid in his voice.

"Well, if you wanted me to play a game with Kiran, it's over, right?"

He snorted. "Is it? You don't know him, then. He'll chase any sentient creature who wears skirts. Hasn't he flirted with you?"

"Not clearly, no. Some comments, maybe. He also thought I had something with you, which I denied."

Larzen laughed and rolled his eyes. "With me. Now he's going to say I'm the problematic one. It isn't true at all. I'm straightforward about what I want. Nevertheless. I need you to go back to the ball. Dance with people. Pretend to be having a good time. Make sure he sees you."

Zora sighed. "What do you wish to accomplish? It's not like he'll break up his betrothal with the princess and choose me. You know that, right?"

"Of course. I just want some confusion. The game isn't over until it's over, Zora, and I still need you there."

Right. As if whatever confusion would accomplish anything. But she didn't have a choice. "As long as I don't have to flirt with anyone, I can do that."

"That's perfect." He kissed her forehead. "You're lovely, you know? If my heart hadn't been taken, you'd certainly shake me."

What was she supposed to say to that? Thanks? It wasn't as if he'd ever be interested in her for anything serious. But there was something odd in what he'd said. She narrowed her eyes. "I thought you were single."

He put a finger over his mouth. "It's a secret. Exciting secret love."

"Good luck, then."

He laughed. "Luck has nothing to do with it. You need to plan."

With his bizarre methods? He was doomed. Still, Zora smiled. "Well, you're on your way to happiness, then."

He looked down, then back at her. "I hope when this is over you'll reconsider your decision to give up on love. Men need to be loved, too."

Be loved. Not love. There was a difference there, and it was funny that he didn't see the selfishness in the way he put it. But she didn't want to argue with Larzen—for many obvious reasons. "I'll think about it," she said with a smile, then walked back to the ball.

If she was supposed to be seen, then she would be seen. Mauro was still at their table. Zora turned to him. "Could we dance?"

He looked at her as if wondering if she was feeling well. She wasn't going to be upset if he said no because he was weird anyway, but he just shrugged. "What for?"

"So that normal guys are encouraged to ask me to dance. I don't want to be sitting."

He paused, then said, "That makes sense."

They got up and he ended up telling her about the parties in the Marshes. They had different instruments and didn't dance in couples. Instead, everyone danced together, entire villages, including children.

"It sounds wonderful!"

"Maybe you could come visit," he said.

Zora smiled then looked down. "I don't know if I'll be allowed out of the Dark Valley."

"Yes, true. Maybe before you go back?"

"Maybe."

He asked her about the parties in the Dark Valley. She

explained that there was never live music and it never included all the adults, since some of them would be busy doing rounds.

"Also, everyone carries swords all the time," she said.

"That's why you carry it on your back, so it doesn't limit your movements."

Zora laughed. "I guess. I'll confess I'm feeling odd without my sword, as if something was missing."

"They let you walk around the castle with it during the day, so that's good."

"Why? They don't let you?"

"No. Only in the practice grounds."

"Interesting."

She had never noticed that. Again they were underestimating her. What if she'd been an assassin or something? Still, she was glad she could carry Butterfly during the day, even if she couldn't have it at a ball.

They sat down and Zora's mind went back to the idea of a place where life was calm, simple, and entire families could celebrate outside at night, without any fear. A place she'd probably never visit. She sighed.

A young man in his twenties invited her to dance. So her idea had worked. He was a rich farmer from the Marshes. Then she danced with a merchant from another region. She didn't like that one. The guy was nice, but his breath smelled of garlic. When Zora sat down, Loretta was nowhere to be seen. Hopefully she was all right. Mauro was no longer at the table or anywhere she could see, so he probably had left the ball, too.

A very tall champion with short black hair approached her. "So you can slay lions?"

That was the opposite of what she had said. "No."

"Oh, you said you could. I can be wild like a lion, too. Raw." He moved his hand as if it was a claw.

What a weirdo. "Excuse me." Zora got up and walked away.

She couldn't see Loretta or even Mauro. In fact, people were leaving already, and she was hoping she had played whatever part Larzen wanted her to play. She scanned the room for him, but she found Griffin, instead, with a cup in his hand. He walked towards her. Well, walk wasn't the right description, more like staggered towards her.

"Con-gratulaaaaaa-tions on your victory."

Zora frowned. "You're drunk."

He pointed at her. "So perceptive. Can I have a dance?"

"You can barely stand."

"You'll dance with Kiran, but not with me. You're all like that."

Zora didn't appreciate whatever insinuations he was making. "I didn't say no. I was just wondering if you could still dance. Being, you know, drunk."

He took her hand but kept holding the cup with the other hand. "You underestimate me."

"It's annoying, right? When people think you're incompetent."

They walked to the center, Griffin apparently oblivious to her comment.

He stared at her. "How did you do it? Tonight?"

"You should know. You did almost as well as I did. How did you do it?"

"Oh, me it's different. Being a monster isn't all bad, you see. Gotta have some upside, too. Do you have a monster inside you?"

Zora couldn't contain her laughter. "I don't know. It depends on what you mean. Maybe." She then remembered the episode in the library. "But monster or not, you shouldn't have tried to prevent me from competing. That was dirty, Griffin."

He stopped and let go of her hand. "All I did was ask you nicely. I assure you that's not talking dirty."

Zora rolled her eyes. "I don't mean talking. I mean locking me in the library."

"I showed you what you asked. What's wrong with it?"

"You didn't lock the door to that room?"

"What room?"

Zora sighed. Either he was playing dumb or perhaps he hadn't done anything. Or maybe he was so drunk he didn't remember.

She tried to remind him. "In the library. You didn't lock me there?"

"Zora, I swear. I don't understand what you're talking about. Dirty stuff, in a room in a library, I swear it wasn't with you."

She grunted in exasperation. "I have no clue what you're getting at. I'm just asking if you tried to prevent me from competing, that's all."

"Why would I? I asked them to do the challenge especially for you. I thought you'd be out tonight."

That was true. She smirked. "You failed."

"Totally failed. Now some visitors want my skin saying the challenge was boring. They want blood and broken necks. You see my dilemma?"

"No." She then noticed that his face had an odd color. Food intoxication was something she knew. "Griffin. I think you're going to puke."

"I sure want to."

If he vomited right there and then it would be too much

humiliation. Especially for her. She didn't give a damn about Griffin. "You might want to go outside. Or to a washroom."

"No, no, no, no. I'm polite. It's rude to leave a woman in the middle of a dance. I know my manners."

"Puking in the middle of a ball isn't good manners."

"I said I wanted to, not that I was going to. You do know there's a huge difference between wanting and doing, right?"

"Not for me." She had to find a solution, fast. "Could you walk me to a garden? I need some air."

He actually looked concerned. "You're not well? What are you feeling?"

"Just need some air."

"Sure."

He guided her to a side door. Zora glanced around for people she knew. Loretta was not there. Larzen was nowhere to be found. Perhaps she was afraid of what people would think, but in reality there were people and couples walking back and forth through doors.

They walked to a garden and she pulled him to a quieter area, with bushes covering them and no people around.

"Sit," she said.

He sat on a small rock and leaned his head on his hands, looking extremely unwell. Some of her longtime instincts from helping her parents' patients were coming to her. "I'll get you some water."

Then he sounded as if he was about to puke. Oh, no, not on that hair. Zora pulled it back. If there was a god of hair, it had blessed him. It would be a blasphemy to get it dirty.

She closed her eyes as his stomach returned its contents on the grass. Some of it spattered on her shoes. Gross. So gross. At least it didn't go on her dress. Griffin then lay down on the grass, just beside the disgusting puddle. She pushed his arm so he wouldn't get it on the sleeve of his jacket. At this point, all she could do was go back inside and get some help for him. This had been awkward enough.

She crouched. "Griffin. I'll be right back. Hang on for a while."

Strange, he was blinking as if dreaming. This shouldn't be a symptom of drunkenness. As far as she knew, of course. She hadn't seen anyone very drunk in the Dark Valley. Either way, he wasn't well.

"I'll get you some help." She touched his shoulder to reassure him, but he pushed away her arm.

"Go away, Alegra. Go to Kiran. Go, go. Not anymore."

Zora felt a chill in her stomach. Could it be? He was interested in Alegra?

9

SECRET

The day she had met Griffin came to Zora's mind. Both the princess and him were at the inn. Could it be? Or maybe it had been just a coincidence. Zora tried to double check if she was imagining things. "Griffin, I'm not Alegra. And she's your brother's betrothed. You know that, right?"

"No. No. You kept saying it was nothing." He paused, eyes closed. "That you didn't even kiss him. I saw your kiss. You're a liar."

He then laughed, still with his eyes closed. This was looking like some side effect of a strange potion. Maybe he had taken a poorly made potion to do well on his task. Or maybe someone had given him a malicious drink. Confusion? Poor sight? She wasn't sure. Or maybe he was just drunk.

"Griffin, this is Zora. Zora, the champion. The one you want out? Remember?"

"No, Alegra. No more." He wasn't listening to her.

At least his volume was low. Imagine if someone heard him calling his future sister-in-law's name. Now, how could she get anyone to help him? Larzen, maybe? No. This was too big of a secret, and information was power. She had to hold it to herself, especially considering everything Griffin was doing against her.

"Can you get up?"

"Never," he mumbled.

Great. Now how was she going to get him away from that garden? She couldn't leave him there babbling stuff that could be quite dangerous. She also didn't want to leave him unconscious and unattended. There weren't shadow creatures in the Gravel castle grounds, but still...

Perhaps some potions could help him. She still had some speed and precision and maybe she could get the ingredients for something for his stomach, so he would get better soon and not risk sleeping then vomiting and choking. That was the procedure. But then, there were the strange symptoms. No, speed and precision should be enough to at least make him get up and walk. All Zora had to do was be fast.

Griffin was quiet and she preferred not to say anything, lest he started talking about Alegra. She re-entered the salon as if she'd only been out for some air. It was good in a way for people to see her and not get any ideas about her and Griffin. Please. She'd be the one to puke.

Larzen was there. She approached him slowly and whispered, "This round seems to be over, don't you think?"

He chuckled. "Far from it. But I guess you want to leave."

"I was visible for a long time."

Larzen sighed. "Go. Leave me here, alone, uncared for."

She laughed because she knew he was joking. "There will be more rounds. I'm your loyal pawn."

"Loyalty is an admirable quality." He took her hand and kissed. "Good night."

She curtsied, hoping she was doing it right, as it wasn't

something she'd practiced, then turned around and walked away. Once there were no people around her, she ran to her bedroom. Loretta was already sleeping. So *that* was why she'd disappeared. At least she was safe. Zora took two small bottles, put the potions she had ready, then took some ingredients and put them in a duffel bag. She sort of remembered where the garden was, so she took another door and reached it from the outside. It hadn't been more than five minutes since she had left. Griffin was there and nothing bad had happened to him. Zora exhaled in relief.

He actually looked beautiful lying down with his eyes closed. No, what nonsense. That was a creepy thought, Zora. She put her arm under his head.

"Griffin, I want you to take a sip of this. It will make you better."

At least she hoped. He mumbled something that sounded like "No." Perhaps she could ask for help now. Right then he mumbled something that definitely sounded like "Alegra" and she remembered why she'd taken upon herself to care for him. Not care. Just get him to his room before anyone noticed what he was talking about.

Zora put the bottle with the speed potion on his lips. "Drink."

"Wine?" His eyes were half open.

"The best wine ever. You won't believe it."

He took the bottle, took a long sip, then threw it. "Not wine."

At least she had extra bottles in her room. And now she had to convince him to take the other potion. "Sorry, I gave you the wrong bottle, this one is the super amazing wine."

She put the bottle with the precision potion on his hand. He drank it. And spat it.

"No, no," Zora said. "Drink it."

"Not wine."

"Of course it's wine. You must have lost your taste or something."

What nonsense she was saying. Still, he drank it and grimaced. "Worst wine ever."

Potions were not renowned for their amazing taste. "Oh, sorry, then. If you get up we'll find some good wine."

It took some minutes, but he did get up. He was still staggering, so she let him put his arm around her for support. Now, she didn't know where his room was. Well, she could take him to his office. She remembered where it was. Sleeping on a rug would be better than sleeping on the ground outside. It was the best she could do. And she was doing a lot, considering everything. She still wasn't sure he hadn't locked her in the room in the library.

The hallway to his office was away from the visitor's section, where Zora's room was, and thankfully was empty. When they got to the door to his office, it was obviously locked.

"Do you have the key?" She hoped she didn't have to leave him in the hallway.

Griffin shook his head and pushed the handle. It had a faint purple glow. So it was enchanted or had some other kind of magic. He turned it and the door opened. Phew. At least they would be able to get in.

"You might want to lie down on the rug."

"Rug?" he mumbled, then led her to the wall with the weapons and touched a hammer.

A wall opened in it, leading to a simple bedroom with a double bed and some drawer chests and cabinets.

"Even better," she said. "Now lie down and wait because I need to make another potion for you."

Griffin lay down on top of the covers, and asked, "What do you care? Go find Kiran."

That was getting annoying. "I'm Zora. The Dark Valley champion. Your enemy." She wasn't acting like an enemy right then, but it was just that she wanted to keep his secret to herself.

Griffin mumbled, "Don't want Alegra."

"You're very lucky, then. Because I'm *definitely* not her." If he kept insisting she was going to slap him.

She touched his forehead to check for a fever. Who knew? His symptoms were weird. His temperature felt normal, though. He took her hand and brought it to his chest, then his eyes opened and he looked at her.

"Zora." He exhaled, as if he relieved, then closed his eyes.

Finally he knew who she was. But then she was wondering how she'd explain being in his bedroom. Whatever. Tomorrow she'd think about it. Perhaps he'd forget everything. She took the ingredients for a potion for his stomach and put them over a drawer chest. There was a book with a dark cover on it, in the corner. Most books had dark covers, of course, but this was completely black, and there was something about it...

Zora opened it. There was a bookmark. The page had a curse on how to turn a man into some sort of monster, but she wasn't sure what it was, even with the drawing. Something with a tail and horns. On other pages, there were different curses on how to cause diseases and even kill a person. She put the book back where it had been, almost regretting having touched it. What was Griffin doing? If he was dabbing with dark magic and maybe even considering using it against his enemies, she would be in a lot more danger than she'd imagined at first.

Chill, Zora. Reading a book didn't mean he wanted to practice those curses. She wasn't even sure if they were real. There wasn't magic like that in Gravel. Or at least Zora thought so. So many things she didn't know.

Now, Zora could walk away and leave him there. She could also... An idea was forming in her mind. She could make a malicious potion to make him sick. But then she'd need to go back to her bedroom and wouldn't be able to come back in.

No, no, that was a horrible thought. What would her parents say? Their mission was to treat anyone who came to them, regardless of who they were. Maybe one day she could give Griffin a potion to impact his performance, but what was the point in doing it now? If he got sick, they'd no doubt just postpone the challenge.

Then there was the way he'd said her name, as if he trusted her. She sighed, telling herself not to dwell on it. He hated Zora. And he was in love with someone else. Not that it mattered, except that knowing it was a weapon in her hands. Unless he did know how to make curses. Then she was doomed.

Whatever, Zora. She made the potion for his stomach. It was also good for overall disposition, and would probably prevent a headache or whatever symptoms alcohol intoxication caused. If she thought about him as a patient who had fallen into her care by chance, she owed him the best she could do.

Once she finished the potion, she touched his shoulder. "Griffin. I have something for you. It doesn't taste great, but it will make you feel better."

"I'm better."

He put his hand over hers. This was so awkward. Maybe he still thought she was Alegra. As long as he didn't tell her to go away, she didn't care.

"Listen to me. You're tough. You can handle drinking something that doesn't taste great. You'll feel better. Trust me."

His eyes opened a little, he moved his head up and drank a few sips, then leaned down again and closed his eyes. With a calm, steady breathing, he fell asleep. Still, Zora stayed there for some time, checking for fever and to see if he had any other strange symptoms. When it was clear he was feeling well and sleeping peacefully, she left.

This was the only thing she'd done since she'd left her valley that would probably make her parents proud. Even her victory was tainted with her cheating potions. If they heard she'd been playing flirting games, they'd be horrified. But taking care of someone who needed, even if it had been his own fault, that felt right.

Perhaps in a way his heart had been broken, too. She didn't think much of men's hearts, but didn't mind doing something to alleviate a person's suffering. Yet Seth was in the dungeons, suffering. But Zora had no choice about that. It was one more thing among so many that she wasn't proud of. And still, all she could do was move forward.

GRIFFIN HAD a pleasant feel in his body. His memories from the previous night were blurry and out of order. Alegra's announcement came to his mind, but it had no bitter taste anymore. Instead, he had a pleasant feel of hands on his hair, a calming voice, someone giving something to him, and sleeping without nightmares for the first time in years. He felt calm, soothed, as if someone had put a balm on his heart.

A hand touched his hair. It was colder now and didn't feel the same. He opened his eyes. Alegra was there. He pushed her hand and sat up. "What are you doing here?"

She looked offended. "Is that even a question?"

"How did you even enter?"

She ran her hand through his hair. "I have my ways."

"Stop." He pushed her hand again.

"What's wrong with you?"

He laughed. "With me? Are you serious? Or are you insane?"

Alegra looked down. "Is this because of last night?"

"Guess."

"Griffin, you know I can't just tell your brother to break up our engagement."

"Of course not." He rolled his eyes. "Maybe you shouldn't have gotten engaged in the first place."

She shook her head. "He insisted. He wanted to announce it during the competition. He thinks it will show strength and unity. What was I supposed to answer?"

"What about 'no, I reconsidered it and don't want to marry you anymore.' Is it that hard?"

Alegra got up. "It's not easy!" She gave her back to him and stopped as if looking at something over his drawer chest. She then turned. "Give me time. That's what we agreed, wasn't it? That he would tire of it on his own and break up the engagement, that we didn't need to confront him. I can't just turn around and tell him I don't want him anymore. He'll want a reason, and I don't want him suspecting you."

Griffin glared at her. "You didn't seem uninterested last night."

"To protect you!"

He sighed. "Maybe. Fine. But I don't want to see you, then. Not like this."

She sat on the bed, her eyes wet with tears. "I was thinking of you. I did this for you. Don't be unfair to me."

"I'm not being unfair. I'm just saying we can wait. Once you and my brother break up for good, then we give it some time, and then we can see each other again."

"I don't want to be without you."

Griffin wasn't even sure if her tears were true or not, he wasn't even sure if she wasn't playing him, didn't even understand why he'd fallen down so low to betray Kiran like that. Still, he tried to calm her down. "I'm just asking you to wait. It's safer for us both."

She rubbed her eyes to dry her tears. "I can wait, I guess." Then she turned to him. "Have I ever sung to you?"

He closed his eyes, feeling exasperated. "Alegra, just go."

Then she started singing. There were no words he understood, just a beautiful melody. He still thought it was super weird for her to be singing out of the blue and was wondering how to make her stop without offending her.

But then he looked at her and noticed how amazingly beautiful she was. So, so beautiful. Entrancing even. And he didn't even understand why he was upset at her. She'd been surprised last night when Kiran announced the engagement and turned her face when he tried to kiss her. More than that, he remembered her hands holding his hair, taking care of him, making sure he was all right. Her soothing voice, her calming touch, the way she helped him get rid of his nightmares for one night.

He pulled her and kissed her. Alegra smiled.

Griffin ran his hands through her hair. "I still would rather we didn't see each other for a while. For safety."

"But I'm already here. If anything, it's better if people don't see me leaving your office early in the morning."

That was true. He hugged her and fell back asleep.

A BLACK SHADOW had his hands on his neck and was strangling him. Griffin was out of air and couldn't scream. He sat up, panting. Sunlight came through the window. A bad dream, like usual. Alegra was gone. He was starting to wonder if he had dreamed all that. As he got up, he noticed a potion bottle on his drawer chest.

So she'd been there. Griffin was confused. There had been this amazing feeling in being with her last night. The feeling that someone truly cared for him. Then, there was something quite odd, but he couldn't put his finger on it.

These questions would drive him to madness. This was silly, stupid, but he saw no other choice. He opened the door leading to his secret dungeon. So many nights spent there, in the company of chains, manacles, and so many books. He also had an enchantment table, with many tools. One of them was the truth basin. He'd never peered on it for anything serious, as there were so many warnings against it. Some books talked about it being used by teen girls wondering if they were loved. Griffin had always thought that was more than stupid. You should know if someone loved you, right?

But now it was his time to be stupid. There was something odd about Alegra. It was if she loved him, but then... He wasn't sure. Perhaps it wasn't as obvious, especially when a person was engaged to another.

He poured a thick viscous black liquid on clear water.

Doing this was risky. False images could have terrible consequences. He knew that. And yet. He couldn't go on like this. Sometimes all it gave were forms with the liquid. Some lucky few claimed they'd seen full visions. Griffin just wanted a clue, a direction, and since he couldn't confide in anyone, he was doing this, knowing the risks and all.

The black liquid seemed to be forming the shape of a woman. Griffin felt dizzy and closed his eyes. Then it hit him. A vision, clear like a dream.

It wasn't Alegra but Zora, tears in her eyes.

She turned to someone, begging, "You have to stop it."

Her voice had such a desperation that gave him chills.

Then she was weeping, her face covered with tears and contorted in fear. "Please!" Her voice cracked with such an urgent plea, fear, and more desperation than he'd ever seen in anyone.

Griffin stepped away and opened his eyes. That dreadful "please" was echoing on his head and he felt horrified at whatever would cause that reaction.

He sat on the floor. Great. Now he had a headache. A headache with a desperate scream. What had that been about? He'd come to the truth basin to ask about Alegra. Why was Zora there? Why hadn't it given him his answer?

He sat there for a long time, waiting for that feeling to subside, that crazy fear and desperation. When he felt calmer, he realized that there was just one logical answer: he was so worried about the Dark Valley girl getting hurt that it was affecting his thoughts. Who knew, perhaps it had been on the back of his mind when he asked the question. And it was a sign, too. Zora had to leave that competition. He wasn't going to allow whatever fate he'd seen happen to her, he wasn't.

Griffin clenched his fists, annoyed. And now he had no

idea about Alegra. But maybe it was true that asking the basin about love was stupid. She'd been with him last night, making sure he felt better. There was no question that she cared about him. It was just a matter of waiting and trying to convince her not to see him for now. That, and keeping his cool. He could do that. Hopefully.

10

NEW CHALLENGE

Without any messages from Larzen, Zora took the morning to walk around the gardens with Loretta. There was a nice, cool breeze. She still remembered what she'd done for Griffin, somewhat incredulous that she hadn't taken the opportunity to let him puke in front of everyone. Where had petty Zora been? But then, she'd learned he'd been interested or even involved with Alegra. Perhaps it would be useful. It was probably neat to be the Linaria princess, beautiful like a heroine in a story, the girl for whom everyone fell in love. It would be nice if her biggest love problem was having to choose between a handsome king and a gorgeous prince.

Loretta didn't seem that happy either.

"So," Zora said. "Met anyone interesting last night?"

Her friend shrugged. "Don't know. I came here for something different, for a chance at... Something greater? Something more than just the people from where I'm from. Perhaps it was a hopeless romantic dream."

Zora tried to encourage her friend. "There will be more balls. It's still early to be disappointed."

"Yes, but if a man is interested, he'll court you early, not wait until his first options are taken." She closed her eyes and sighed.

"You danced with so many good-looking men," Zora insisted.

Loretta shook her head. "The only one who wanted to see me again was Ephemerus."

"Oh. I thought you disliked each other. He's handsome, though."

Loretta sat on a bench and leaned back. "But what's the point? I didn't need to come here to meet him. It costs a lot, you know, to be one of the important guests like I am."

"But it's fun, isn't it?"

She looked down. "I don't know."

It was weird to see Loretta like that. Zora sat and rubbed her hand on her friend's back. "There will be better days. And nights."

"Ephemerus proposed."

Wow. Surprising. "Is that a problem?"

Loretta was still looking down. "He's my competitor. I know that he wants this alliance to get rid of my shop."

"Maybe he likes you."

"Yes, but... That shop, it was my mother and me. She worked so hard, so hard. I thought it would allow me to have my freedom, allow me to be the master of my destiny."

Zora understood the need for freedom. "Maybe you could just stay single."

"But I want love!" She got up, then sat down again. "Maybe I thought I could marry a poor champion. But then he'll be interested in my money. And if I marry someone richer, then they'll see me as their property. If I marry Ephemerus, I'm giving up all that my mother fought for."

Zora took her friend's hand. "I understand your dilemma. But try to listen to your heart. Maybe you like him. Maybe you could keep your shops separated. Or you could strengthen each other. Maybe you don't like him, in this case, you're beautiful, friendly, smart, and rich, and will always have plenty of possibilities. Give it some time."

Loretta was silent for a while, then said, "You are right. I think trying to rush these things doesn't end well. It's just, being here, it's my only chance to meet new people." She stared at Zora. "What about you?"

She took a deep breath and looked away. "I don't want to fall in love again. I want freedom."

"Are you sure?"

Zora shrugged. "Well, I think so."

"Maybe when you go back home?"

She was going to explain that there were very few available young men in the Dark Valley and she disliked most of them, when she saw someone approaching. Her stomach formed a knot.

Alegra smiled at them. "Hello. If it isn't the two most beautiful ladies in the festivities."

Zora snorted.

Loretta laughed. "That's too kind of you, and definitely not true. Congratulations on your engagement."

"Yes." Alegra looked down, a dreamy face. "I can barely believe it myself."

Zora wanted to punch her. Yes, maybe Griffin was in love with her and nothing had happened between them, but he did seem disappointed and betrayed. It was unfair that people like Zora and Loretta had to suffer for love while Alegra was loved by everyone and yet breaking hearts.

Still, she didn't want to show what she felt, so she smiled. "Our king is wise and made a wonderful choice."

Alegra sat by them. "Yes. But is it a great choice because of the alliance with Linaria? Or is it for me?"

Loretta chuckled. "What a question. He'd need to be blind not to choose you."

And yet maybe he was blind to certain things. Zora now wanted to strangle the princess and she had to keep those feelings in check.

Alegra shook her head. "You're too kind. What about you, lovelies? Don't tell me you were breaking hearts."

Zora grunted. "Breaking hearts is not really my thing."

"I was joking." Alegra touched Zora's shoulder. "I was just wondering if any of you had your eyes on someone."

"Nobody yet," Loretta said.

"I do. I got my eyes, heart and soul set on..." Zora smiled. "The Blood Cup. That's going to be my husband. No risk of breaking my heart."

Alegra was thoughtful. "I think a cup would be a she."

"My wife, then." Zora waved her arms.

The princess nodded. "You do make a good case for a relationship with objects."

Loretta was laughing. "She's joking."

"No, no," Zora protested. "I'm quite serious."

"Hum..." Alegra said. "Could it be you have your heart set on a certain prince?"

Zora rolled her eyes. "I might be naïve and from the Dark Valley, but even I know that it would be dumb. A prince wouldn't exactly want *my heart*, but something else, which I'm not giving."

"Giving can be fun." Alegra shrugged. "And frankly, it could be a great opportunity for a girl like you."

A girl like her? What was she implying? Zora took a deep breath to calm herself. "Larzen has helped me find accommodations and any contact we have is because I'm a champion and the sole representative of the Dark Valley. That's it. Any other assumption is absurd."

"Larzen." Alegra seemed surprised, then she smiled. "I was just asking! An innocent question. And being honest in my advice."

Zora got up. "I need to train. Would you mind if I leave?"

She barely heard what they said while she left. Her head was fuming. Just being around Alegra got Zora on edge, and then it was almost as if the Linaria princess was mocking her. And it made no sense. She was a princess, soon to be queen, why would she waste her time with the likes of Zora and Loretta? There had to be something there, but she couldn't figure out what.

LARZEN HAD Zora meet him behind the same tapestry where they'd spoken during the ball. It was evening already, and until then she had been thinking he'd forgotten her or abandoned whatever plan he had, now that Kiran was engaged.

She arrived first and felt like a fool, hiding there, plus it was a dark place that made her uncomfortable. After some time, she heard steps and saw the prince's face, half breathless, as if he'd been running.

"There you are." Larzen chuckled. "Tell me, what did you do to my younger brother?"

What? Could he know what had happened? But Zora recomposed herself quickly to hide her shock, pretending not to understand. "Why?" She tilted her head and smiled.

"Griffin wants you out so bad. It's funny."

Zora smirked. "I'm thinking he's a sour loser." And an ungrateful bastard, but whatever.

"Maybe. Maybe knowing that someone beat him at something got him over the edge."

"But this is bad news, right?"

Larzen shrugged. "The same. I think he would still have tailored the challenges against you. Next one will involve horse riding and climbing."

Zora's stomach sank. "I don't know how to ride a horse."

"Aren't we glad you'll have a day and a half to learn? Also, the climbing, I think they'll set it up in a way that your height will put you at a disadvantage."

Of course. She was the shortest champion. Still. "But it can't be all based on height, or Griffin will be doomed, too."

"Well observed. Still, they can make it just high enough for him. I think there will be a wall with places for you to put hands and feet."

"Higher than I can reach."

He nodded. Zora looked down, thinking. Maybe she could use a potion of strength to jump. Jump up and hold herself? It sounded hard. She wasn't that strong in her arms. An idea came to her mind. "Will I be allowed to bring weapons? Or some accessory?"

Larzen narrowed his eyes. "I think I see what you're thinking. Would your sword help you?"

"Yes!" Butterfly was stronger than any sword she'd seen in Gravel City.

He nodded. "I think I can convince them to allow that. We need a spectacle, after all."

Zora was a little more relieved. "What about riding? Is there any way I can practice it?"

"Yes, go to the stables at six in the morning tomorrow and

after tomorrow. Look for Renan, he's a stable boy. He'll help you."

"Great. Any requests for the, you know, other game?"

He smirked. "Not yet. But I'll let you know."

THIS TIME when she entered the arena, Zora's heart was noticeably accelerated. The competition was in the late afternoon, when the sun was still up. She was already tired, though, having spent the last day and a half learning the basics of horse riding. Renan was a sweet teen, and the whole thing hadn't been awful, but she was still far from a decent rider.

The upside was that she had learned where they kept the horses that would be used for the competition, and, just to be safe, put a calming potion in their water. The idea was that this way, the experienced riders wouldn't be able to do much better than her. She also wanted to make sure the horses wouldn't run too fast, jump, or anything like that, as she was still somewhat afraid of falling.

She also had no clue what kind of climbing she would have to do, how much it would slow her down, and her odds at not being eliminated. This would also be the first time she saw Griffin since... Since he'd puked on her shoes. She wondered if he remembered what had happened, and if maybe he was aware that she knew his secret.

At least the champions had to bring their swords. Having Butterfly on her back made her feel safer.

Again, the contestants stood in a semi-circle in a corner. Her eyes met Griffin's. He frowned at her, looking upset. *You're welcome, Griffin.* Next time she'd be happy to let him puke in the middle of the ball.

Zora had considered blackmailing him about him and

Alegra, asking him to stop trying to get her out of the competition, but she had no proof. Who would believe her? All she'd accomplish was make him even angrier. It did hurt a little to know she had worried about him and the only thanks she got was a nasty frown. It shouldn't hurt, though. It didn't matter. All she had to do was win the Blood Cup. Right. As if she could even get past this challenge. That was something else causing her dread; the idea of coming back to her valley and letting everyone down. It couldn't happen. She had to find a way not to be eliminated.

The presenter explained the task. The horses would be assigned to them at random. She knew that part. They had to do six turns around the arena, then climb a structure that had been built in the middle. She had no idea what the structure would be like. In the end, they had to go to a fenced area where they had pigs, kill one with their sword, and present its heart on a table in the middle. That was weird and gruesome. Of course, there were ten competitors and only eight pigs. The last two champions to arrive there would be eliminated. Then the last two to put the hearts on the stands would be eliminated, too. That was an interesting way to add blood to the competition. She wondered if it had been Larzen's idea, since he had promised to make sure this challenge would require a sword. Still, four champions would be eliminated. That was a lot. Perhaps the goal was really to get Zora out, even if her performance were mildly decent.

A champion on her side whispered, "You know, the pigs are innocent, too."

She just sighed. It was true, though. And not all these champions would know how to kill them fast and mercifully. But she couldn't think about that. Maybe one day they'd do these games without animal cruelty. So far, at least it had been human-cruelty free, and she wasn't going to complain about that. She also figured they had chosen pigs because there were none in the Dark Valley. But she wasn't too worried about that part of the competition. They shouldn't be harder to kill than shadow wolves. Her issue was whether she'd make it to the pen in time.

The horses were numbered, and they pulled papers with the champions' names. Zora got number five. That was Pipa. That mare wasn't the nicest but wasn't the most difficult either. A good choice.

Zora stood by her horse, waiting for the signal to mount. To her surprise, Alegra came to the grounds and greeted the champions. She stopped by each one, wishing them good luck. When it was Zora's turn, she held her hands and smiled. "I hope you win."

Zora snorted. "I just hope I don't get eliminated."

Alegra shook her head and touched Pipa. "That's a lovely mare. I'm sure you'll do great."

A chill down Zora's spine made her turn. Griffin was glaring at her. Perhaps he was imagining that they were laughing at him, like friends gossiping. Imagine if Zora told Alegra that he got drunk and kept calling her name like a pathetic fool. She wished she could be capable of something like that because he deserved it. But then, one reason she wouldn't do it, other than self-preservation, was that she didn't like Alegra either. Perhaps she and Griffin were perfect for each other. The mere thought made her sick.

Alegra moved to the other competitor, and still Griffin glared at Zora. Shouldn't he be looking at the princess? Oh, right, "no more," he'd been saying. Perhaps he thought that if he glared at Zora enough, she would screw up her performance. Right. But then, that nasty book in his bedroom came to her mind and she shuddered. Could he do something like that, though? So annoying. As if having the challenge tailored to her weaknesses weren't enough.

Life wasn't fair, and expecting fairness would be dumb. It was just that it hurt to realize that her shots at winning the Blood Cup were not so great after all. Perhaps the idea that belief would affect her results was dumb. What use was believing when she'd have a lot more trouble to climb the structure than her competitors? The structure. She couldn't see it very well from that distance. But it didn't matter. It was always better to focus on one thing at a time, and for now, all she wanted was not to fall from her horse and hope the other competitors didn't go much faster than her.

An assistant helped her mount and adjust the saddle. Pipa seemed jumpy. Weird. Maybe it was just because of that enclosed space. Zora had an odd feeling that something was wrong, but it was likely just her fear plus knowing how slim her chances were for this challenge.

A bell rang, and all pen gates were opened at once. Pipa was galloping, and quite fast. And Zora was terrified, grabbing on the saddle as if grabbing for her life. After a while, the mare started to jump, as if trying to buck Zora off her. Zora tried to rub the mare's neck, as if to calm her, but it was worse. Eventually, Zora slipped, so that she was holding herself on the side of the saddle. She could barely breathe, so afraid she was. Zora pulled herself up and leaned on the saddle, holding herself with all her strength, with her legs and arms. She wasn't sure if she was moving forward or where the other champions were. All she wanted was not to fall. Could it be that she'd made a mistake on her potion? No, no way. Zora was a very precise potion maker. It was just some spooky bad luck that she got a crazy horse. What on earth was wrong with Pipa?

Still, at least she was moving. And jumping. When Zora thought she had crossed the finish line some two times, they waved the black flag, meaning she had finished her race. Already? She pulled the reins to stop the mare, which made her rear, so that Zora fell behind Pipa, but the mare moved away from her and some assistants proceeded to restrain the horse.

Zora had hurt her butt from falling, and her legs and arms were sour, but the worst was her fright. Trembling and feeling nauseous, she took a few slow, deep breaths, then proceeded to the climbing structure. Or structures, as there were several identical ones, probably so that there would be room for all the champions.

Uh, oh. This was not her lucky day. She had imagined that there would be some kind of wooden wall where she could stick her sword and use it for support. But no. The first structure was like a ladder, but with giant spaces between the steps, taller than a person. The sides were made of metal. Yeah, Butterfly was sharp, but Zora would not be able to stick it there. Even the first step was out of her reach. Great. But she could reach it by jumping. The tricky part was bringing up her body. Actually, she grabbed the bar close to the metal edge, so that she could step on the sides for support. Then she crouched on the bar, and jumped, then used the side to bring up her legs, and crouched again. Thank goodness she had been used to exercising her arms in the Dark Valley. It was pointless to learn skills with a sword if your arms got tired after a few swings. Still.

Zora paused. And looked. Relief came over her. The competitors had not gotten to the climbing structure yet! Some horses were trotting around the arena. She had a chance. More than a chance. She could win this challenge. In the end, the crazy horse had helped her.

She continued her climb. There was loose sand on the bottom, but she hoped not to fall. Her arms were trembling when she got to the top and rang a bell.

Then she had to jump to a lower platform, then another lower platform. There was a cable to cross over a gap. Two cables. Of course, the idea was to step on one cable and hold onto the top cable. As Zora got to the edge and raised her arms, she realized the obvious: she couldn't reach the top cable. Now, she thought her balance was pretty good, but not enough to walk on a cable without support. But hey, they hadn't said anything about walking. Zora knelt on it, holding it with her two hands, knees, and her feet crossed below it. This was going to be slow, but at least she wasn't going to fall.

As soon as she left the platform, her body turned, so that she was hanging on the cable. No matter. Her legs were tightly wrapped around the cable and she pulled herself with her hands, even if the cable was above her. This wasn't too bad. Again they had underestimated her. Then she noticed, from the corner of her eye, someone crossing a cable. Griffin. But it didn't matter. As long as she didn't get eliminated, she didn't really care. Of course, winning would be better, but what could she do?

Once she finished the cable, there was a normal ladder to go down. There were other competitors in some pens already. No kidding. Zora got in a pen, and with a swift strike, beheaded her pig, trying to imagine it was a shadow wolf. It wasn't and it felt bad to kill such a large animal, but she had to ignore that feeling. They had probably added this step thinking she'd be squeamish. They had underestimated her. Again.

She cut the pig open quickly, took the heart, and ran to the table. She was second. After Griffin. The audience cheered for her. Her clothes were bloody and disgusting, but she guessed that was what the crowd wanted.

Griffin approached her and whispered, "In my office. In one hour."

Zora was startled. What was that about? But she couldn't exactly say no and just smiled. "Sure."

Then she saw Mauro getting the third heart and waved at him. He ignored her. Well, he had said they weren't going to be friends in the arena, it was just that she had imagined it would be only when they were competing. Perhaps he was just really focused.

This time they didn't have to wait for the other champions, so Zora ran to the bath house to get rid of those clothes and that blood.

She dreaded meeting Griffin. Perhaps he'd find an excuse to kick her out of the competition once and for all. Perhaps it had to do with Zora knowing about his feelings for Alegra. Zora had no clue. She leaned back and put her hair in the water, trying to see if it could cool off her thoughts.

STAVOS APPROACHED HIM. "What do you think?" the assistant asked.

Griffin pretended to be surprised. "About what?"

"That horse, running like that. The other horses, trotting slowly."

Griffin shrugged. "The girl got lucky. Or rather unlucky. She almost fell."

"So you don't think we should investigate it?" Stavos insisted.

"What do you believe you'll find?"

Stavos raised an eyebrow. "If the girl is using dark magic, she should be eliminated."

Griffin waved a hand. "Dark magic! You need to learn a little more about horses. What did you expect, putting them in this arena with people yelling? Of course they would behave strangely."

"Horse riding was your idea, your highness."

"And it was a stupid idea, as we clearly saw. Now, if you excuse me, I need to wash."

Griffin walked away. The games committee would likely discuss what had happened, but the final word was his and his brothers'. He didn't think either Kiran or Larzen would want anyone probing on dark magic or insinuating that anyone was using it in the games. Hopefully.

11

DARK MAGIC

Zora was wearing tight pants and a white shirt as she walked towards Griffin's office. Her heart was galloping. His door was open, but still she knocked on it.

"Come in and close the door," he said from a corner.

She did so, and found him sitting on the same armchair, hair wet, dripping on the loose tunic he wore. She stared at the weapons on the wall.

"Your highness wanted to see me?" She said as she sat. Tum, tum, tum, her heart was so loud, she hoped he couldn't hear it.

He tilted his head and narrowed her eyes. "I think you realize you could have died today, right?"

Zora leaned back. This wasn't exactly what she'd been expecting. "Well, that makes it a day like any other in my life in the Dark Valley."

"Really?" He was surprised. "I thought you kept lights on, you made sure creatures didn't spawn."

"There's always a mistake somewhere, and they come from the forest."

"Can't you stay indoors? Build a fence around the village?"

Zora shook her head. "Fences don't stop them. Not even doors do for long."

"But I'm sure there must be a way."

That was annoying. "For sure. Perhaps your highness would like to go there and offer your precious advice with more wisdom than all the generations that have been living there. Perhaps that will save us."

He leaned back and blinked. "I didn't mean that. Anyway. You almost fell from that horse. I saw you. You were terrified. Is that true?"

What was she supposed to say? That no, she was an amazing rider and enjoyed the experience? Her shoulders sagged. "It's true."

"Now, did you charm that horse hoping it would make you win the race?"

What? A horrible chill ran down her spine. "No. You said it yourself. I was terrified. I was."

"Perhaps you made a mistake."

Zora got up. Nothing made sense. It didn't make sense that there would be any magic like that. "No. I don't know how to charm or curse anyone or anything living. You can research. The only magic we use in the Dark Valley are potions and enchanting objects for strength, durability, and things like that. We would have no use for enchanting animals. There aren't even horses in the Dark Valley. All we have are chickens. How would I even know that?"

He shrugged. "Perhaps you tried something you didn't know well. It clearly went wrong."

This was such an unfair accusation. "I wouldn't try something crazy like that. All I know how to do are potions, and between the time they picked my horse and when I mounted it, there wouldn't have been time to give it to it."

He nodded. "And yet you knew how to ride. How so?"

"I practiced this morning and yesterday."

Griffin leaned forward. "How did you know you'd need to ride?"

She had the answer for that at the tip of her tongue. "Well, it's obvious, isn't it? You want me out of the competition. There are no horses in the Dark Valley. I realized the challenges would be tailored against me when the first one was in the dark."

He snorted. "Which you won."

"I did. And I guessed there would be riding and I was right. I should have found a way to grow a little. Unfortunately, I didn't think of that."

Griffin smiled but then took a deep breath. "That horse had dark magic, Zora. I promise you I won't let them know about it, but I need to understand what happened."

Zora sat again and crossed her arms. A horrible idea came to her. Could it be? It was the only thing that made sense. "Fine. You want to know what happened? Well, dark magic isn't used in Gravel. With exceptions, maybe." His dreadful book came to her mind. "But perhaps people from outside the kingdom know how to use it. Like the only person who touched my horse and wasn't their caretaker or me."

He paused for a moment then laughed. "Alegra? Why would she curse your horse?" He didn't seem aware that Zora had heard him calling her name.

"I have no idea." And it was true. Maybe Zora was imagining it just because she didn't like the princess, and yet, it was the only possible explanation. She continued, "But if you are saying it was dark magic, and it seems you understand about it, and I know it wasn't me, then there's only one answer." Zora shrugged. "Unless you cursed me with your stare."

"My stare." He shook his head. "It's not even possible to curse anything with a stare."

"I don't even know what's possible or not, but if you know so much about it, maybe you can figure out who did it."

Griffin was silent, looked down, then looked back at her. "You guarantee you used no magic on your horse? If ever, I hope it doesn't come to it, but if ever you have to swear or we need to use something to make sure you're saying the truth, you guarantee it?"

"I didn't use any dark magic and I have no clue how to use it. I can swear it any way you want it." She made sure not to say *no magic*, after all, potions were magic to some extent. But he was obviously talking about whatever had made Pipa act like a crazed horse.

Griffin nodded. "I believe you." He looked down for some time, as if thinking, then said, "I might have been mistaken. Perhaps it was the agitation in the arena that caused that mare to flip."

"I thought you... your highness was sure it had been dark magic." Zora had to know if someone, probably Alegra, was trying to kill her or something.

"No. I was just checking. And testing you."

What an asshole. "Oh."

"But you were still in danger." His dark eyes were on her. "The visitors are going to want to skin me alive if you get hurt. You could still quit this competition. Quit it while there's time, before anything bad happens."

Zora trembled. "Is that a threat?"

"No! No. Of course not. Last thing I want is seeing you hurt, in case it wasn't clear."

"Of course it's not clear. You don't want me to get hurt, I have a groundbreaking suggestion: stop stacking the challenges against me. Had I been a little less strong on my arms, I could have fallen today in that stupid anti-Zora climbing structure. Unless you want to convince me someone cursed it. Yes, there was sand at the bottom. But still, it would be a fall from a considerable height. And that structure was planned to make me fall." Zora was almost crying in anger. This was so unfair.

"I didn't know it was going to be like that. I only give suggestions for the challenges." He looked down. "But your point is fair. I promise you that, from now on, the challenges will no longer be designed against you. But you have to promise me that if you feel you're in danger, if anything strange happens, you'll seek help, you'll quit if it comes to it. Don't forfeit your life for a stupid competition."

Zora frowned. "You're in it. You know it's not stupid."

He closed his eyes and sighed. "Zora, in my case it's my life." He stared at her. "Not in your case. Today, for example, you could have called for help, you could have signaled you were in trouble, and yet—"

"I was too busy making sure I didn't fall." She rolled her eyes. "I know, it sounds weird that none of those things crossed my mind while on a crazy jumping horse."

His eyes were calm when he looked at her. "There will be no more horses."

She remembered that moment in the night he had felt sick, when he'd opened his eyes and said her name as if relieved. But she'd better forget it. He had obviously forgotten it, which might be for the best. "Thank you."

He nodded. "You may go now, unless you'd like to discuss anything else."

Zora noticed his expression. No, this wasn't a hint to whatever she had heard. "It's fine. Thank you for listening to me."

He smiled. "Any time."

There was something so soft and pleasant about that smile. Zora turned quickly, before she started noticing anything else positive or captivating about Griffin. A few days ago, she'd faint if a prince smiled at her like that. Now, it was all different. Still, weird how he had acted almost as if he didn't hate her. And he definitely didn't remember that she had taken care of him and given him potions that night. In a way, it made her sad. She hadn't helped him because she wanted some advantage. Still, she thought maybe it would mean a truce between them or something. On the other hand, he would perhaps know that she had heard him calling Alegra, and that could be quite dangerous. So there was an upside to that.

THERE WAS another ball that night, and Larzen had given Zora a bright red dress.

"Oh, wow. This is Amazing!" Loretta said when she saw her.

But her friend looked beautiful, too, this time in a silver dress. "You also look great."

As they got to the ballroom, it wasn't as full as the other night. Mauro was sitting at a table and signaled for them to sit.

Zora was happy that their trio would be together again, and that his strange behaviour in the arena hadn't meant anything. They had barely sat when Ephemerus invited Loretta to dance. Oh, dear, this wasn't going well.

When her friend was gone, Mauro said, "Zora, I'm sorry."

"For what?"

"I thought you had cheated."

"Oh."

Mauro looked down, as if embarrassed. "Your horse was the only one that ran. But Stavos explained how it made no sense that you would have done anything. You almost fell, right?"

"I did. It was terrifying."

"I hope they start doing some normal challenges, some basic sword fighting or something."

Zora smiled. "Me too."

"I bet being from the Dark Valley you'll be skilled, fast, and strong with a sword, but clumsy."

She was curious. "Why clumsy?"

He shrugged. "You fight monsters, not people."

"Maybe." Mauro was definitely smart and observant. Zora then said, "You do believe I didn't cheat, right?"

"I think there was no way you could have done it, there would have been no time. But there is another factor people didn't notice. You weren't so slow in the climbing, and you were quite fast at killing the pig. Faster than me. You wouldn't have been eliminated even if you got a slow horse. And that climbing structure was harder for you than for all of us. So in the end it wouldn't matter."

"Neat. I didn' pay attention to the other champions." She paused. "Which is quite dumb, now that I'm thinking about it. Don't you have some saying about it?"

Mauro laughed. "Fail to measure your competition, and you'll soon be measuring your failures." He paused. "But it's tricky. We also have: focus too much on the enemy, and you'll lose sight of your own path."

Zora chuckled. "Perhaps the solution is balance."

"Maybe."

They were quiet for some time. The king and the two princes arrived and sat in their designated area. Alegra was there, too. Zora avoided staring. She still got chills down her spine thinking that the princess could have cursed her mare. But why? Why would she do that? Then something else hit her. How Griffin had changed from sure that there had been dark magic to dismissing it completely once she suggested it could have been Alegra. If he was really in love with her... Perhaps he could be trying to protect her. Perhaps he had truly perceived dark magic. But it still didn't explain why the princess would have done it. Unless... unless she knew that Zora had heard Griffin calling her name. But how would she know that?

Right while these thoughts circled in her head, Alegra walked in their direction, smiling. "Congratulations on both of you for passing your challenge."

Mauro nodded. "Very kind, your highness."

"Thanks." Zora wasn't going to call her 'your highness' because she wasn't a Gravel princess or queen. At least not yet.

Alegra didn't seem to mind, as she reached her hands towards Zora, who pulled them and hid them behind her back. "Oh, sorry. I was eating and they're all sticky."

"Like I would mind." She then put her hand on Zora's shoulder, which was terrifying, too, if she were to do any weird magic. "You were amazing tonight. That was some horseback riding."

"I'm glad you enjoyed it." Zora smiled but watched the princess for her reaction.

"For sure. You're my favorite." Alegra turned to Mauro. "Sorry." She then turned back to Zora. "Remember that if you need to talk to someone, I'm here. You can also go sit with us."

She glanced at Mauro. "Later, maybe. I'll leave you two to discuss your victory."

She then left.

Mauro had his arms crossed and spoke at a lower volume than usual. "Is it just me or is she weird?"

Insanely weird, and it was good that Zora wasn't alone in her opinion, but she wanted to hear his. "Why do you think that?"

"Why would she act as if she were your best friend? No offense. She's not like that with other people."

That was a good point. "I haven't figured that out yet. I agree it's a bit odd."

"And we'd better not mention it in public, especially..." He gestured towards something with his head.

Kiran was walking towards them, and addressed Zora. "May I have a dance?"

Weird. Zora had been pretty certain that he wouldn't dance with anyone else now that he had announced his engagement, but she wasn't going to say no.

As they got to the middle, Zora said, "Congratulations on your engagement, your majesty."

"Not *your majesty*. Aren't we poetry pals?"

"I didn't know that."

He shrugged. "I'm saying it now. Gotta appreciate a lady who knows her love words."

This was getting awkward. Zora wanted to change the subject. "You made a lovely choice for a wife."

"Hum. You mistake choice with duty, dear."

That was a very nasty thing to say if he wanted to imply he didn't really want to marry Alegra. Zora hated that princess and still got upset at him for her sake. But she just smiled.

"Great duty. Alegra is gorgeous and Linaria can be a great ally."

"So they say."

Zora had no answer.

After some time, he said, "Amazing riding in the challenge."

"Thank you."

"Are you going to tell us your tricks?"

"Trick to making a horse crazy and almost fall? I don't know that."

He took a deep breath. "There were some... suspicions." He smiled. "I didn't let any speculation go very far. But if you do have special skills... Our kingdom could use them. You could have a good position and fortune."

Zora shook her head. "I only know potions and enchanting objects, that's all."

"Perhaps we could discuss your potions. They have their uses, too. Depending on what you can do. The offer stands, Zora."

"Offer?"

"Stay in the castle, as my... magic advisor. How's that?"

Zora remembered how Seth had told Razi that he wasn't going back and how she thought he was selfish. But there was a workaround. "If I could come and go, between here and the Dark Valley, that could be possible. I wouldn't want to abandon my people."

"Your people... that's so cute. You speak like a queen."

"No. Certainly not." Zora glanced around to see if Alegra was looking at them. Perhaps it had been jealousy that made her curse her horse, if it was true that she'd done that. But the princess wasn't around. Griffin, on the other hand, was staring as if he were trying his evil eye again. After their talk, she didn't think he had done anything, especially because he seemed concerned, but still... Then she thought that maybe he was glaring at the king, not her, since he had stolen Griffin's beloved. He should try to be more subtle.

"What a wandering eye," Kiran said.

"I fear your betrothed could be upset that you're dancing with someone else."

He laughed. "She'd better get used to it. If she gets upset with just dancing, she's in for a shock."

Zora looked away. This was way too uncomfortable.

Kiran said, "That was a joke, Zora."

She rolled her eyes. "Right. That was hilarious."

"We may differ on humor but I hope we can find other common ground. You will be my potion girl, right?"

"I need to think about it."

Kiran frowned. "Wow, what a tough decision. What part of living in the castle, being pampered by attendants, and earning money is the issue?"

"The part where everyone has more power than I do and think they can control me."

"You're coming from the wrong assumption that you're powerless."

She smiled. "Sure. Just let me think. I like to ponder my decisions."

"Remember I can order you if I want. But I'm nice. I enjoyed watching you today immensely. I wouldn't mind more of that."

"I thought you were interested in my potion-making."

He shrugged. "It might include some occasional riding. Don't worry. I'll enjoy teaching you."

"I'm done with riding."

Kiran smiled. "Then it will be my pleasure to change your mind."

Zora didn't reply and was happy when the song was over. Loretta was dancing with someone, and Zora told Mauro she was leaving. When she passed Larzen, she glanced at the exit, hoping maybe he would follow her.

He joined her behind the tapestry in a few minutes.

She said, "Can I go now? I danced with Kiran."

"You look troubled. What happened?"

Zora thought for a while, then decided to be honest. "He was saying he wanted me to be his magic advisor, his potion maker. I'm not sure if he was implying also... He said some things with double meaning."

"He's playful, but if he wants you to work for the kingdom, you should consider it."

"Now you don't think he goes after every woman he sees?"

"Well, he likes to have pretty girls around him and that might be behind his decision to have you in the castle, but frankly, he has so many options... He's not going to worry if one girl isn't interested. He'll just move on."

"But if he was flirting, that's completely gross, with Alegra right there."

"You said double meaning, right? So technically it isn't flirting. I think he's just being playful."

"I'm also afraid of upsetting Alegra..."

He shook his head. "No. I don't think she cares that much, especially if it's only innocent dancing and talking."

"I guess." Zora almost wanted to mention the incident with the horse, but decided it was better not to. "And what about your game? Where is it going?"

"Just keep being yourself; aloof, dry, and uninterested. I might ask you to go to a certain place, attend an event, and then I'll let you know. And tonight... I'd rather you stayed. But I guess leaving is intriguing. So you can go."

Zora smiled. "Thank you."

Yay, how awesome it was to have someone telling her where and when she could go. What a situation. But then, Larzen had helped her. Still, she feared what he would demand of her. There was only one thing she could do: figure out where Seth was. Without Seth, Larzen had no power over her. She would still collaborate with him, but only up to a certain point.

As for Kiran, she wished she could make him start ignoring her. His invitation to be his advisor sounded quite fishy. And Griffin... If he was going to stop making the challenges anti-Zora, that was great. She didn't mind his glare or the fact that he still probably thought she had no shot at winning the cup.

As she got close to her hallway, somebody appeared from behind a vase, knife in hand, pointing at Zora.

12

ASSASSIN

I t was a man with a hood over his head with holes for the eyes. With her left arm, Zora moved his knife hand away from her, punched him with his right hand, while kicking him. As he contorted in pain, she reached for the knife and kicked it behind her, since there was no time to pick it up. She kicked him in the ribs, but he pulled her leg and dropped her on the ground.

Still, from the floor, she tripped him, got up, and ran backward to reach the knife. As he advanced on her, she blocked him and stabbed him on the shoulder and ribs. The man then turned around and ran. He probably could still win, but perhaps didn't want to take any chances or get hurt in the process.

Zora stood there with a bloody knife in her hand, then ran to her room and blocked it from the inside. Loretta would have to knock.

She was trembling as she sat on her bed. If it had been two people, she'd be dead now. All because she wasn't carrying Butterfly. Who had sent that assassin? Alegra? No, there was no point. It could perhaps be another champion. Stavos had warned her. She should have listened.

IN THE MORNING, after pondering a lot, Zora decided to talk to Griffin. Why Griffin? Well, no way she was talking to Kiran. Larzen would want something in exchange for whatever help he gave her. The younger prince was the only one who would listen to her and not ask for anything in return. Well, he would ask her to quit the competition, but at this point she was getting convinced that he'd just keep asking, and she could deal with that. And she didn't have to tell him everything.

It had been just a matter of asking Tania, her attendant, and she got an appointment for ten in the morning. Earlier than she expected.

This time the door was closed, and he opened it for her after she knocked. He was wearing just a leather vest and pants, no shirt, like in the day she'd first seen him. Zora moved her eyes towards a giant axe on the wall.

"What's going on?" he asked as he sat in his usual chair.

Zora sat across from him. "Well, last night I left the ball early—"

"Was there something wrong?"

"In the ball? No. I was just tired. And, it was foolish, but I came to my room alone. In theory, nobody can enter the castle, right? Still, I'm a champion, even if you don't think much of my chances..."

He rolled his eyes.

She continued, "And Stavos said some competitors could maybe resort to violence when nobody is watching and—"

"What happened?" He was leaning forward, eyes intent on her.

In a way, it was better to let them know that there had been an assassin in the castle. She exhaled. "A man attacked me with a knife. In the hallway. Near my bedroom."

Griffin widened his eyes. "Are you hurt?"

"Not really. I took his knife and stabbed him on the shoulder and ribs. Then he ran."

He paused as if taking in the information, then asked, "What did he look like?"

"I don't know. He had a hood and was dressed in black, very plain outfit."

Griffin sighed and leaned his forehead on his hands.

Zora said, "Please, don't kick me out of the competition."

Griffin shuddered and looked at her with a horrified expression. "Is that what you're afraid of? Not competing anymore?"

"That's one thing. But I'm also scared for my life. Not in the arena. Outside. Had it been two people last night..." She looked down.

"You would have gotten hurt or maybe wouldn't even be here."

Zora had rather been thinking she'd obviously be dead, but it was true that there was a small chance she could have defended herself. Perhaps Griffin didn't underestimate her *that* much. "Exactly."

"Any idea who could have done it?"

Well, Zora suspected Alegra, but wasn't going to mention it. She shook her head.

"Do you still have the knife?" he asked.

She had brought it, yes. She took it from her bag and handed it to him, rolled in a handkerchief. It was a beautiful knife, with an intricate handle. "I didn't have time to wash it."

He shook his head. "It's fine. Can I keep it?"

"Yes." It wasn't as if Zora could do anything with it other than maybe wash it and keep it for herself, but she wouldn't want to carry a murderer's weapon.

He got up and put the knife on a table, then said, "I'll be on the lookout for anyone with the wounds you described. You said shoulders and ribs. Do you remember which side?"

Not really. Zora closed her eyes and tried to remember the motion of her hand. "I stabbed him with my right hand, so his left side."

"So you stabbed the shoulder from the front, not his back."

"Yes."

He sighed. "I see. Well, this is something that can happen to champions, but nobody should be able to get in the castle." He exhaled. "I'll assign two of my guards to watch you. They'll rotate the hours. If you need some time alone or whatever, you can dismiss them, but make sure to meet them as soon as possible. I'll also have your lock changed. It should be enough. Still, from now on, you must carry your sword wherever you go."

"What about when I have to wear a dress?"

He shook his head. "Find a way to carry it. Or a small knife, anything. As one of the finalists, you're a target. There's more security in the house of champions." He was thoughtful. "But then there's security here, too. I don't understand."

"Me neither." But Zora was surprised at how his response was meticulous. "But thank you."

He was lost in thought, then said quickly, "It's my job to look out for the champions." He turned to her. "I'll leave you in the training grounds. It's a safe place with lots of guards. Once you get your assigned escort, you can leave if you want to."

"Thank you."

He shook his head. "It's my duty." He thought for a moment, then said, "There was something I wanted to ask you. What does my brother want with you?"

That question caught her unaware. Zora almost asked, "Which brother?" but then caught herself in time and asked instead, "What do you mean?"

"You were dancing with Kiran."

Zora shrugged. "I guess because I'm a champion? He wanted to congratulate me." She didn't want to give him more details than she should.

"Be careful. You're worried about your physical well-being, and that's great. In fact, it was my mistake for not having foreseen it earlier. But there are other ways you could be hurt. Don't trust my brother. If anything, you should avoid him."

"Don't worry." She rolled her eyes. "I'm not... naïve. Or dumb."

"I'm not saying that. Even smart people sometimes fall into traps. Of course you can say: I know it's a trap and I won't get caught, but maybe the best solution is to stay away from the trap. It catches you unaware, Zora."

"All I did was dance with him. It's not like I can say no when he asks."

"What?" He laughed. "That's absurd. Who said that?"

"I... it's general manners, isn't it?"

He frowned. "No. No. Of course not. You can say no to anyone you want anytime you want, even if it's the king of the universe. That includes dancing, or talking, or sitting. Anything. You can give an excuse if you want to be polite, but you don't have to dance with anyone if you don't want to."

As if crossing the king were a good idea. "It's not a torture."

"If you like it, then fine. But if it gets uncomfortable, step away. Come talk to me if he acts in any way that's inappropriate."

Interesting. Perhaps he wanted some reason to split Kiran and Alegra? Zora decided to check Griffin's reaction to the topic. "Well, he's engaged to the most beautiful woman I've ever seen. I doubt he'd be interested in being... inappropriate with anyone else."

"First, you need to see more women. Second, you clearly don't know Kiran. I do."

Zora shrugged. "Whatever he wants, I'm not interested."

"Well, but he's not going to be that direct, that's the point. He might say he wants to offer you a position at court or something, and from there he'll work his way. That's what I mean."

That was useful information. "So if he were to say he wanted me to work for him, I should refuse?"

"Yes. He's done that to other girls. Then kicked them out once he got tired of them or if they didn't want to do the type of work he wanted." He looked at her. "If you do want to stay here at the Gravel castle, you know that all the champions are offered a position either in the castle guard or other forces. You can find a place here."

He sounded sincere and it didn't sound bad, but still. "I don't want to abandon my valley, though."

"It makes sense. We can figure something out. I'll want to visit it, you know. I missed it last time."

Because he was probably with Alegra. Anyway, it didn't matter. "We'll be happy to have you there."

He smiled. That smile. That was a dangerous smile, and it was a good thing Kiran didn't have it. Zora stared at a sword on the wall. It was beautiful, probably made in copper, and quite ancient.

"You like it?" he asked. "It's a relic from the period before

Gravel. If you want, you can come some other time and I can show you some of these weapons. I'm running a little late now. Can I accompany you to the grounds?"

Zora was still stunned at how nice he was. "Sure."

They walked mostly in silence and he left her in the gate leading to the grounds. Mauro was there with two guys from his team, and introduced them to Zora. The champions could have people helping them, but these assistants weren't allowed in balls or inside the castle. The two guys were polite, but she left them to their training. Sword fighting. Was Zora really clumsy at it? She didn't know, and just sat at a bench, waiting. There was another champion with a team of three people running laps.

It could have been any of these people attacking her last night. Except, how had they gotten in the castle? Not even the other champions were allowed there, only wealthy visitors, like Loretta. Now, it couldn't have been any of those visitors. Rich people paid others to do their work. It had to be someone who worked in the castle or who had gained entrance somehow. Perhaps it was pointless to try to figure it out. Maybe Griffin would find something. Right. As if he'd waste his precious time looking for Zora's assailant. She had to remember that, for the royal family, she was nobody. That included Griffin, even if he had been nice.

A blond girl walked in the grounds and then approached her. "You're Zora, right?"

"Yes."

"I'm Natasha. I'm going to be one of your guards. The Royal Guard sent me."

"Oh." Zora hadn't imagined it would be a woman, but it made sense, in a way. The girl wasn't much taller than Zora but she probably knew how to defend herself and others.

"Thanks." Perhaps what confused Zora was that the girl was wearing a dress. "But... you work like that?"

She laughed. "Not usually. But I was asked not to draw attention. That way it will look like I'm your friend."

"Smart."

"I guess. So... do you want to train or do you want to go somewhere else?"

"I need to find my roommate. Other than that, can you fight with a sword?"

"Well. Yes." Natasha grimaced.

Of course. "I mean... You could use something else to fight. I want to practice it and I was wondering if you could help me."

"Sure. Sounds fun. We'll just need to get some practice swords."

"Nice."

That was going much better than Zora had imagined. She just had to remember not to trust the girl completely, as she reported to Griffin, who wanted Zora out of the competition.

GRIFFIN FELT as if trying to carry a load too heavy for him, while at the same time trying hard to control himself not to explode. Riding in the forest usually brought him a sense of peace, the feeling that he could just take off and go anywhere he wanted, that he had the world at his feet. But now he felt as if he had a chain dragging him. Since his parents had died, nothing had been the same. Three brothers, committed to keeping the kingdom in peace, and yet, he felt it was falling apart. But then perhaps it was just Alegra. Or just him. He was the one who had been foolish, who had been betraying his brother.

He tied his horse then sat on a rock and stared at the ruins of what must have been a temple a long time before. Alegra had been curious about it when they had passed it the other day. Hopefully she would remember how to get there. If she didn't show up, it would be both a disappointment and a relief. He took a leather band and tied his hair in a ponytail. Its movement with the wind didn't usually bother him, but somehow now it did. Perhaps it was just that he wanted things in control.

After a while, he heard hooves then saw a horse with its rider on it. Alegra dismounted and approached him. "So you finally have some time for me? Be careful because next time I'm the one who'll be too busy for you."

"I don't doubt it."

She tied her horse on a tree, then turned to him. "You've been distant. Is it that cup that's taking your mind?"

"I have to be distant. You're engaged, Alegra. It's almost as if you forget it."

"I do. It's so pointless that I forget it." She looked at him. "You tied your hair."

"It appears to be the case. So," he began cautiously. "What did you think about the last challenge?"

"Bloody and disgusting." She grimaced. "Whose idea was it?"

"The pigs? Not mine. But the castle kitchen used them."

She chuckled. "Great. You can be a butcher if the whole prince thing doesn't work out."

Griffin smiled. "I'll keep that in mind. It's always great to have options." Then he changed his tone and veered the conversation in the direction he wanted. "And what did you think about the race?"

"The horses? It was all right. I don't know, I thought those games would have more dangerous challenges."

He observed her. "So you'd like to see me in danger?"

"Not you. You're good. The others."

"It's bad enough when there are wars, to draw blood from the enemy. I'm not hurting any of my subjects." He paused and stared at her. "I guess you wouldn't mind seeing any of the champions hurt."

"Oh. I didn't mean that. I meant more danger. They're all skilled, aren't they? The best in the kingdom?"

"Not necessarily. Who knows how each region chooses their champions?" He decided to be more direct. "I have a question for you. Why did you stop by each contestant to talk to them? Why did you touch some of the horses?"

"My duty, as future queen—"

"Future queen." He snorted. "Good to know."

Alegra sighed. "I don't mean that. I'm trying to establish good relations with your people. It will be the same if I marry you. Why do you think I choose to do something in *your* competition?"

"Convincing, Alegra."

"No, I—"

"But can you answer my question? Why did you do that?"

"Still got mud on your ear? I just explained it."

Griffin took her hands in his and was tired of this game. "True. Except you didn't explain the part where you cursed Zora's horse. Why did you do that?"

She tried to pull her hands but he held them. "Why?" he insisted.

"Where are you getting this nonsense from?"

"I know dark magic, Alegra, and I know it was you. I just want to understand why."

She pulled her hands and clenched her fists. "I have no idea what you're talking about."

"You do, Alegra. You do very well. And let me be clear that if you do that again, I'll make sure you answer for it. Do you know what our people used to do with suspected practitioners of dark magic?"

"VERY WELL," she roared. She stepped back. "YOU'RE ALL MONSTERS."

He was startled and speechless.

She then looked down, as if sad, and changed her tone. "I read... some stories. I was horrified, that's it. But Griffin, instead of obsessing about the Dark Valley girl, you should rather worry about beating her. It will be ironic if she ends up with the Blood Cup, won't it?"

"She can't beat me." He wasn't worried about that.

"That's the humble Griffin I know."

"But it's true." He sighed, still thinking about her outburst. "We're not monsters anymore. At least *most* of us. But we do serve justice to people who try to commit murder either by magic or by hiring assassins." He watched her reaction.

She just waved a hand and laughed. "Murder. Let's not get that far. And even if you got stuck with your crazy idea, what would you do? Antagonize Linaria?"

"You're a tiny kingdom with enemies on all sides and a weak army. If anything, *you* shouldn't want to antagonize us."

She stood near him and ran her hand on his arm. "Well, I don't want to antagonize you."

"Then tell me the truth and explain why you did it."

Alegra paused for some time, then took a deep breath. "I meant no harm, I swear." She sounded as if she were about to cry. "It was just, she's the only woman in the competition, and you were being really unfair to her, trying to get her eliminated. I wanted to help her. But it wasn't dark magic. I just thought it would make her horse go faster. I'm so sorry. So sorry, Griffin." She covered her face with her hands.

Her explanation didn't convince him. He was starting to wonder if Alegra had also sent the assassin. "Are you by any chance jealous of her and Kiran?"

Alegra removed her hands from her face and rolled her eyes, as if offended. "No. First, I'm not jealous of him, second, if I were to feel jealous, it would be of someone who actually had a chance at winning his heart."

She wasn't going to confess, of course, so there wasn't much more for them to discuss. "Fine, then. But I don't want any more interference with the champions or the competition." He went back to his horse, thinking that he would need to keep a closer watch on her two assistants and even check if any of them had knife wounds.

"Griffin, you're leaving? I thought we were going to spend time together."

"I think you should give my brother a fair chance. I don't want to stand in your way to being a *queen*." He couldn't hide the bite in the last word.

She smiled and shook her head. "If you insist on leaving, I'm gonna have to play dirty."

"Go ahead." What could she do? Get undressed? It was her solution for everything, except he'd had enough of it. He thought back about all their times together and cringed at the shallowness of it all, at her fakeness, how much she'd been manipulating him, and how naïve and gullible he'd been. Just the thought hurt.

Then she could be trying to hurt Zora, and her desperate

"please" from his vision still echoed in his mind, was part of his nightmares, was like a chronic pain. And it could have to do with Alegra.

Griffin was already on his horse when he heard it. The most amazing sound. He turned and couldn't stand seeing his beloved there, so sad. His only thought was to apologize to Alegra. He would do anything to see her smiling again, the woman he loved.

THE SECOND GUARD had arrived early for her duty. Her name was Isabelle, and she had dark brown skin and beautiful curly hair. They had convinced her to do something that a few hours before Zora would have thought impossible. She was riding with them and Loretta outside the castle walls. They were just trotting, though, but Isabelle was up ahead.

"Slowly," Zora yelled. "Remember I'm still scared."

"That's the point," Natasha said, her blond hair flowing with the wind. "A good experience will make you forget the bad one. So you won't be traumatized."

Loretta was looking around. "These woods are so beautiful."

"They are!" Natasha said. "And there are quite a few lakes around here. We could go for a swim."

Zora wasn't sure about the idea. "What if someone sees us?"

Isabelle had fallen back, and asked, "What? You think swimming is a crime or something?"

"I mean seeing us undressed." Shouldn't her concern be obvious?

The black-haired guard shrugged. "Well, you try to keep an eye and ear out, that's all."

"I think I'll pass," Zora said.

Loretta still had a huge smile. "Next time we need to plan better and do a picnic."

"If we know in advance, for sure!" Natasha said. "I was glad to take a break from city duty, but I didn't think it would be this much fun."

"You might still have to stand outside or wait around for me to do something." Zora looked down, thinking that it wouldn't be fun like this all the time. "Sorry."

Isabelle laughed. "It's our job, silly. And we're happy to make sure the only female champion stays alive. Anyway, where are we going?"

"We could still see a lake," Zora said. "Or even better, a river. Is there one around here?'

"Aw," Natasha groaned. "It's all the way back."

"What if we went somewhere with a view?" Loretta suggested.

"Rooster peak?" the blond girl asked the other guard.

"Sounds good." Isabelle nodded. "We can also stop at the Mystical Ruins."

"Mystical?" Loretta laughed. "This is getting interesting."

"Ooooh, you're going to be sooo mystified." Isabelle didn't hide her sarcasm.

Zora laughed. It was so good just to go out, have fun and forget all the other stuff happening in her life.

They stopped and dismounted near what looked like a destroyed building, with stone walls, only openings for windows, no glass, and no ceiling. Funny that the construction style was similar to the houses in the Dark Valley. And that reminded her of the privilege of being in Gravel city and its surrounding woods.

Zora turned to the others. "Thank you so much. At home, we can never relax like this in the forest, there's always that fear..."

Isabelle put her hand on Zora's shoulder. "You're safe with us."

"Thanks," Zora smiled.

Loretta stared at the structure. "I thought this was going to be bigger."

Isabelle shrugged and smiled. "Told you."

"It's actually pretty long," Natasha said. "Do you want to check it out?"

"I'll stay with the horses," Isabelle volunteered.

"I can stay, too," Loretta said.

Natasha seemed disappointed, then turned to Zora. "You?"

"I'd love to see it."

The guard smiled.

The ruins were more like the rests of a line of buildings. "Do you know what this was?" Zora asked.

"Nobody does. I guess that's why they say mystic. Not that it's anything, well, mystifying." She chuckled.

"It's interesting." For the most part there wasn't much inside, they were just empty structures.

Natasha pointed farther ahead. "In the end there, there's a part with more rooms and even dungeons."

Those were very dark places and Zora still feared what could grow or spawn there. She smiled and shook her head. "Too dark for me. I can look at it from the outside."

"I get it."

They kept walking by the ruins. The last building was indeed bigger than the others. Zora shuddered imagining what would be like inside it, the memories of the Dark Valley and her fear of dark places so deeply ingrained in her.

Once they turned around the building, Zora saw two horses tied to trees.

"We'd better turn around," Natasha whispered.

At first she didn't understand the girl's precaution if there were only two people, but on a second look, Zora noticed that there were clothes on the ground nearby. There was something familiar about them. It had to be an impression. Or maybe not. Zora would go crazy if she didn't check, so she approached the pile.

Her stomach knotted. She could recognize that vest and pants anywhere. Griffin. The dress was white with some embroidery on the collar. Nothing special in it, except that she'd seen someone wearing a dress with that embroidery before: Alegra.

13

Zora felt as if she had swallowed something heavy and sticky, and her legs trembled. She ran back to Natasha and whispered, "Yeah, we'd better go back."

When they had given enough distance from the clothes and horses, the guard said, "They're probably nobody important, or they wouldn't be so careless. But still, you don't want to mess with that type of stuff when a lady is involved."

"Can you not tell anyone what we saw? Just in case... Let's say it is someone important, and let's say it's something they wanted to keep secret..."

"I won't even tell Isabelle."

"Thanks." Zora nodded. There was something else bothering her. "Are you going to tell Griffin what we did and where we went today?"

She laughed. "No, no. We report to our superior, Irene. We weren't asked to spy on you or tell anyone what you're doing. Don't worry about it. All we have to do is show up and as long as you don't complain and don't end up dead or hurt, nobody's going to check what we're doing."

"Really?"

"Yes. We were assigned to protect you, not watch you."

Yes, that made sense, and still...

Natasha added, "Think of it this way: they want to keep you safe because you're a champion. It makes sense. But you don't have any secrets, you're not from a rival court, there wouldn't be any point in checking on you."

The girl had a point. "You're right," Zora conceded.

After that, the girls went to Rooster Peak. It wasn't really a peak, or else the horses wouldn't have gotten there. It was more like a low hill. Still, it had a tower. From there they could see the castle, the top of some trees and some lakes.

Despite the beautiful view, Zora's outing had been ruined with the memory of Griffin and Alegra together. How could she have been so dumb? It wasn't as if she didn't know about them. She knew it! And she knew it could have been the princess behind her horse's strange behaviour and perhaps even behind that assassin. And yet, she had gone straight to Griffin. Zora might as well have gone straight to Alegra. She had sought the prince following her gut feeling, something that had never deceived her. Until now. Lesson learned.

When they returned, Natasha went to the city, and Loretta and Zora went back to the castle with Isabelle. The guard stopped by a locksmith for the new keys to her room, but only stood outside the room and then the bathhouse. Zora wished she could go with them, but the girl said she couldn't let her guard down.

After their bath, when Zora opened the door to her and Loretta's room, someone was already there: Alegra, sitting on a chair, wearing that same white dress that had been on the grass. Zora's hand instinctively moved to the hilt of her sword.

The princess smiled. "I wanted to check how you two were.

I heard about what happened. That you even had to get a new key." She showed a key in her hand, then got up. "Rest assured, girls, whatever happens with the royal family, whatever concerns are brought to them, they concern me, too."

Zora glared at her. "I noticed how close you are to the royal family, especially Griffin."

Alegra smirked. "Yes. He mentioned your fears and suspicions, and I got worried."

Zora glared at the princess. "I see. I can imagine how those things could worry Kiran, too. I might bring Griffin's dealings to him."

"Except you won't." Alegra tilted her head. "Because you're nothing. And nobody will believe you."

"I can take my chances." Zora swallowed.

Alegra got up and was so close to Zora she was whispering. "You know what eats you alive? How you wish it was you instead of me."

Zora rolled her eyes. "Oh, yes. My dream is to be a guy's plaything."

"Silly of you to assume he's the one playing. And it's so much fun. Fun you'll never have. Love you'll never have." She sighed. "Anyway. I have your key and I'll be happy to watch out for your safety." The princess then left.

Alegra had said those things on purpose to hurt Zora, so she had to ignore them, except that her words had hit their target. It was true that she was nothing, and perhaps true she'd never be loved.

Loretta had thankfully been quiet during this exchange, but now she stared at Zora. "What in the kingdom was that?"

Zora wanted to answer, wanted to give an explanation, but instead, she sat on a bed and started to cry. She didn't even know what those tears were about. Feeling betrayed? Not able to trust anyone? Knowing that her life was in danger and nobody could help her? She wasn't sure.

Isabelle entered the room. Zora calmed down, dried her tears, then told Loretta about the assassination attempt and ended up telling both of them her suspicions about Alegra, even if she couldn't explain why the princess would do that. Loretta was a little upset she was only learning about it now.

"I didn't want to worry you," Zora said, "And I was the target, not you. And now we have Isabelle and Natasha for protection."

Loretta was still upset. "And what was that last part about? *You wish it was you?*"

Not even Zora had understood that. "I don't know. Maybe she's jealous of the king, which is absolutely ridiculous." On the other hand, it sounded as if she was talking about Griffin, but why would she think Zora wished it was her? It made no sense. She then added, "I never..."

"I know," Loretta said. "She must be paranoid or something."

Zora nodded. "The issue is this room, now."

"You can bar the room from the inside," Isabelle suggested.

"No. I don't trust it," Zora said. "She was here. Someone else could have entered, and done anything. Even something as simple as putting some poison on the pillows, I don't know." She turned to Loretta. "Let's pack. I'll ask Stavos for a room in the House of Champions. It's not as nice, but..."

"You could also go to the city," Isabelle suggested. "My aunt has an inn. I could ask her if she could maybe give you a room."

"But aren't the castle grounds better protected than the city?" Zora asked.

"Not for you, right?" Isabelle said. "There's security in the good inns, too. Only guests are allowed inside. You'll also have your sword and you'll have me or Natasha."

"Can we bar the rooms from the inside?" Loretta asked.

"Yes, you can."

Loretta looked at Zora. "Let's pack." She turned to Isabelle. "And don't worry. I can pay." Then again she turned to Zora. "But next time tell me everything. I mean everything."

"I will." Except the part about Alegra and Griffin, of course. "And I'll pay you back when I get my stipend."

"Don't worry about it."

The sun was already setting when Zora, Loretta, and Isabelle got to Gravel city. It was just a ten-minute walk from the castle, and yet, it was like stepping in a different world. It was so lively, with painters, musicians, artists, people walking to and from inns and taverns, that it felt more like a big party than just a city.

Loretta seemed to have the same opinion, and laughed. "We should have left the castle earlier."

"I guess we were in boredom central." Zora chuckled.

"Oh, yes, it's always a lot of fun when we have the games or other festivals," Isabelle said.

They got a room at Isabelle's aunt's inn, The Wild Boar, but decided to go for a walk instead of having dinner there. In the castle, they used to eat in a designated area for guests, almost always empty. Now they could enjoy the buzz of the city, eat in a restaurant, see more people. At least this time there were no lost children, perhaps because it was night, perhaps because it wasn't something that happened often.

The three of them ended up having a stew at a tavern. It wasn't fancy, but Isabelle had told them it was good. And it was. Loretta had some wine, but Isabelle didn't, since she was technically on duty, and Zora didn't drink. Now that she thought about it, not drinking might have also saved her life when she'd been attacked the previous night, as she still had sharp reflexes.

As they walked back to the inn, Zora noticed a painter selling his artwork on the street. One of the paintings had a strong young man with dark hair parted on the side and a sword. That had to be Griffin, but the painter had exaggerated his muscles, which was impressive, considering they were already exaggerated. There was also a portrait of King Kiran and Alegra, both of them very elegant and beautiful. Zora also saw some portraits of the current champions, even Mauro, who looked strong and fierce in his painting.

"Maybe we should go." Loretta's voice was tense.

Zora's hand instinctively moved to the pommel of her sword and she looked around, but saw no threat.

Then she saw it. Or rather, them. On the other side, there were more paintings. One of them depicted a woman hanging on a cable with a very arched back, head leaning back, and closed eyes. She wore brown leather like Zora had worn for the competition and had hair with dark brown roots and blond tips like her, but she had a lot more chest and she looked more as if she were doing something, ugh, something different with the cable. There were two more paintings of this weird woman that looked like Zora. One of them with her legs wrapped around the step of the climbing structure, and the other with fewer clothes, lying down in the mud. Zora felt her eyes stinging, tears of anger wanting to burst.

"It's unfair," she told her friends. "They don't depict the male champions like that. And she doesn't even look like me." She wiped a tear. It turned out she *was* crying.

"It's men's fantasies," Isabelle said. "They are very visual.

Of course, it would be nicer if they kept it to their imagination."

"Did I look like that in the challenge?"

"Of course not. But notice how the paintings of the guys are not realistic either," Isabelle insisted.

"They look strong. I look..." She didn't even know what to say.

"Lovely ladies," a dark-haired man with a goatee, wearing a suit, said. "Can I help you?" He then noticed Zora. "You don't like your portraits?"

"Of course I don't." She glared. "I don't look like that. And my experience with that cable wasn't quite as... pleasurable."

The man sighed. "I have a family to feed. Those paintings sell. But you're my favorite contestant."

Zora rolled her eyes. "I can see why."

"No. My daughters like you, too. You mean something to them. Look." He took a painting from behind the others. It had a girl with dark hair with blond tips, wearing black leather, holding up a red cup. "Do you like it?"

Zora shrugged. "It's better."

"I'll add some details to this. Come back tomorrow. I'll give it to you as a gift."

"I don't need a painting."

"Oh." The man looked down.

"I can buy it," Loretta said. "It's beautiful."

Zora was still annoyed, and decided to say what she'd been thinking. "Would you like it if someone painted your daughters like that?" She pointed to the other paintings of her.

He looked at pictures. "Yes and no. I think it would be uncomfortable to see people depicting them like that, but at the same time, if people were painting them, it would probably mean they were doing something worthwhile, something that made them recognized. A few stupid paintings wouldn't change that."

Zora frowned. "So you're saying your paintings are stupid?"

"Very much." He laughed. "But it's nothing more than what's already in people's heads."

"Men's heads," Loretta said.

The painter shrugged. "They're clients. If you come tomorrow, earlier, you might find more artists. There are a couple female painters. You'll get a different feel, then."

Zora still hated those paintings, the man, and whatever perverted clients he had, but there wasn't much they could do.

They were tired when they got to their room. Which was good, as Zora fell asleep fast instead of having troublesome thoughts circling in her head.

GRIFFIN WAS GOING INSANE. Or else his mind was manufacturing excuses and trying to erase his mistakes. Such an enabler mind. Parts of the day had been lost from his memory. Or suppressed. Normally, the idea of blackout periods would terrify him, as it could mean that the worst was happening. But it didn't seem to be the case now. He'd been with Alegra and at no point did she act like he'd been out of his mind or about to kill her. So it wasn't that. And he didn't know what it was. Weakness and excuses were the only possible explanations. Perhaps Griffin should be relieved. Still, the idea of not knowing exactly what happened or how things happened was scary, too.

He did remember clearly making some choices that still made him cringe. Why was it that he forgot all his decisions when he was with Alegra? He'd promised himself he'd never touch her again, at least while she was still with his brother, and yet. Perhaps the only solution would be to avoid her completely. But he'd met her just to confront her about security in the games. To confront her about what she'd done to Zora. Perhaps it worked. Alegra had promised not to do it again.

There was still the issue of the assassin. Thinking back on it, his suspicions about the Linaria princess were quite absurd. She'd have no reason to want a champion dead.

Griffin got up to take a look at the knife—and it was no longer on his side table. Someone had taken it. But how could they have gotten into his office? Unless he took the knife somewhere else during one of his blackout periods. All these moments without memories. The logical explanation was that he'd put it somewhere else. Except that he had no idea where.

NATASHA SHOOK HER HEAD. "This is supposed to represent a real sword, not an axe for chopping wood."

"Ha, ha. So funny. As if I hadn't noticed the difference. Let's try again."

Zora attacked the guard with the training wooden sword, but the girl blocked her blow.

They'd been at this for some time, on a meadow close to the city. Zora was awful at parrying. Actually, awful wasn't even the word for it. After all, she had never practiced fighting against a skilled swordmaster, just against mindless monsters. And it showed. Zora was fast but would leave openings for her adversary.

An awful feeling was coming to her. The idea that one of the challenges would include sword fighting had sounded promising. Having trained with a sword since before she could walk, Zora had been sure she'd be amazing. Now, doubts were eroding her confidence.

Zora sat on a rock. "I think I need a break."

"All right," Natasha said.

This was actually a problem in training with her guard. Since Natasha was at Zora's service, she wouldn't push her, tell her not to rest, or anything that a good teacher did. Pushing your limits wasn't meant to be a comfortable experience and sometimes students needed someone poking them.

"You're lost in thought," Natasha said.

"Thinking about the Dark Valley. I was a teacher."

"Nice. Well, as you can see, I don't have any talent to teach anything." The guard laughed.

"You're doing great! You've given me good advice. I guess... I'm just feeling a bit down." Zora hated to admit that, but it was true.

"What do you do when your students are feeling like that?"

"Me?" The memory of dozens of alert, hopeful eyes warmed Zora's heart. "Well, we had a war cry. Not really war, of course. I guess a motivational cry. I always thought that the kids had to believe in themselves, had to trust that they could defeat even a shadow wolf. It meant that they would fight back if the worst happened." Zora looked down, now with some bitter memories. "Because it did happen."

"Let's do it, then. Teach me."

Zora hesitated, thinking it would be silly, but on a second thought, perhaps that was exactly what she needed.

After some practice, Natasha got the hang of it.

Zora asked, "What do we do?"

"WE SHINE OUR LIGHT," both replied.

"What if shadows come?"

"WE FIGHT, WE FIGHT, WE FIGHT."

"What if fear shows up?"

"WE ALWAYS TRUST OUR MIGHT."

"And what do we do meanwhile?"

"WE HOPE, BELIEVE, AND TRY."

Zora sat and laughed. It felt good to yell.

Natasha then asked, "Why does it end in *try*?"

Zora shrugged. "It was the only word that sort of rhymed. And it's for the kids, you know. Sometimes they want to give up when something's hard, so..." She sighed. "I used to think that with enough hope and belief, everything was possible."

"You don't think that anymore?"

That was a huge question. "Not really. But I do believe that hope prevents us from despairing. Especially when things are hard. So I cling to hope. Even if I'm not sure it makes any difference."

"What do you hope?"

Zora took her training sword and started drawing circles on the earth. "A world without shadows, without walls around my valley." She looked up at Natasha. "But this is making me sad. Can we go back to yelling?"

The blond girl laughed. "Of course. I think I'm liking it, too."

"You sure got the hang of it." Zora started again: "What do we do? WE SHINE OUR..."

Natasha didn't join the cry, and pointed behind Zora.

She turned, and saw Griffin walking in the meadow, clapping.

14

SWORD FIGHTING

Griffin was wearing a white shirt under his vest, which was a miracle.

"This is great," he said. "I got a good one, too. What if someone wants to kill me? I'll go to a desolate place. But how will they find me? I'll yell really loud. Why leave the castle walls? Because I want to die."

Zora just stared at him. "You'd better leave the cry-creation for me. Your stuff is dreadful."

"It's horrible. Do you think I like it?" He crossed his arms and yelled, "What's wrong with you?"

"You're not yelling at the right person," Zora shot back.

"Why did you leave the castle? Anyone could kill you. And yes," he gestured towards Natasha, who was standing stiff, looking elsewhere, "you have guards now, but that doesn't mean you shouldn't take precautions."

"You gave the key to my room to Alegra! I know you like her, but—"

"What?" He frowned. "What are you saying?"

"I'm saying Alegra had the key to my room and got in

there. I mean, I understand you trust her. Good for you, but I didn't feel safe there."

He still looked perplexed. "The only person who had the key was the locksmith, who was told to give it to you only."

"Then your security sucks," she yelled.

Griffin shook his head. "No way Alegra has the key."

Now he was going to call her a liar? The image of them together crossed her mind. Zora was so angry she threw the training sword in his direction. It hit his temple.

He put a hand over the spot where the sword had hit him. "What's with you and unprovoked violence?"

Zora regretted it. "I'm sorry. I thought you would dodge."

His eyes were wide. "Who throws things at people hoping they'll dodge?"

"It was meant to release my anger, not hurt you." She approached him. "Can I see it?"

Griffin removed his hand and looked away. The wound was already swelling. Had it been on the other side, his hair would cover it, but it was right where he parted it.

"I'm so sorry," Zora said. Then she added, "But you still shouldn't have given the key to Alegra."

He sighed. "I didn't give it to her. If it's true she has it, I don't know how she got it. But you should have told me."

"Well, no!" Zora waver her arms in irritation. "How could I trust you?"

He was thoughtful for a moment, looked down, then back at her. "You're right. Don't trust me. But I still don't like you out here, just the two of you. And where are you even staying?"

"I'm not gonna tell you."

Griffin paused for a moment, then said, "That's fair. Still, during the day, try to go to places with more security. The training grounds, for example."

Zora didn't want to go there. "I... wouldn't want the other champions watching me training."

"I saw you two sparring." He rolled his eyes. "It's not like you have any surprise moves."

Zora clenched her fists, then something he said hit her. "How long have you been here?"

He shrugged. "A few minutes."

"That's creepy."

His eyes were doing the death stare again. "Better me than an assassin with a poisoned arrow, don't you think?"

Zora was going to retort something, but then, if he'd been there all that time and they didn't notice it... She exhaled. "You made your point. I'll avoid empty places."

"Thank you."

"Why do you even care?"

"You're one of my champions. I already told you that if you get hurt—"

"People will skin you alive. I doubt it, but I get it." She then lowered her voice. "Did you find out anything?"

Griffin shook his head. "Nothing yet. My people checked the castle workers for the wounds you described, even the women. Nothing matches. We'll keep checking."

Zora was surprised. "You got them all checked?"

Griffin scoffed. "It might not look like it, but an assassination attempt within the castle walls is a big deal."

"Thank you."

"Don't thank me. Be careful. You don't know who's after you, you don't know why they are doing it, you don't know if they might have allies. You need to stay alert."

"Fine, fine." She hated having to concede defeat and admit she had been wrong. Then she noticed the bump on his forehead. "I'm so sorry for that. Do you want me to put something on it to heal faster?"

He looked at her for a moment, then shook his head. "I deserve way worse than that. Don't worry. I'll accompany you to the city. And rest assured, I won't check where you're staying. You're right not to trust anyone." He turned to Natasha. "You are?"

She bowed. "Natasha Green. City guard, your highness."

"What's your assignment?"

"To protect the champion."

"So please remember it," he said. "And keep it to yourself. Don't tell anyone where she's staying or what she's doing. Is that clear?"

"Yes, your highness."

He turned to Zora. "Let's go."

She hated that he was making her feel like a child caught doing something wrong, when he was the one doing wrong stuff. Very, very wrong stuff in remote places. At least she kept her mouth shut.

But she had to agree with his point about an assassin. Somehow Zora had been so afraid of Alegra she didn't consider that the princess could maybe have allies or hire more people, and while it was hard to enter the castle, anyone could be out there.

And yet Griffin was telling her all that but had given Alegra the freaking key. Or not. Maybe she'd gotten it through other means. Right. As if they hadn't spent time together the previous day. How could the princess even know about a change in keys if he hadn't told her? Zora had to remember that for all his pretense at being worried, he was still Alegra's lover. And that was insanely dangerous.

They were walking in silence, Natasha after them. It was so

weird how she'd turned into this silent guard, but it made sense that she'd keep decorum in front of the prince. Or behind him.

He stopped when they were on the edge of the city, then looked at Zora. "Is it true you don't think hope makes a difference?"

She felt irritated and humiliated that he'd heard something so private and wasn't even ashamed of admitting it. "I'm pretty sure eavesdropping is bad manners."

"I didn't want to interrupt you, you were focused on training, then talking. But is it true?" he insisted. "You don't believe in hope?"

"Well, if hope and belief made a difference, there would be no shadow creatures in our valley. None of my students would die or get hurt." The memories were painful. Tears were running down her eyes. Stupid tears. "Sorry, I know I said I wouldn't cry."

"If you got hurt. This is different." He searched his pockets. "I... wish I had a handkerchief."

Zora laughed even if she still had tears in her eyes, and jumped at the chance of changing the subject. "You don't even wear shirts most of the time. This is an improvement."

He looked down at himself and laughed. "I have to get better at looking princely, I know." He turned to her. "Now, about your valley, I promise, once these games are over, once things are calm over here, I'll help you find a solution. There must be something."

"That's a nice promise. But remember you can't even keep a key secret."

"Yeah, I'm worthless. You're right."

"I didn't say that."

"I'm saying it. Goodbye, Zora. Stay safe."

He turned around and walked away. Natasha stood there, stiff and quiet.

Zora turned to her, "You're gonna just stand there, like a guard?'

"It's my job."

"I guess." Zora walked back to the inn with a bitter taste in her mouth. She had hurt Griffin and felt bad about it, but it was true he deserved it.

Perhaps it was just that the only person who behaved like an ally was in love with a girl who probably wanted Zora dead.

"SOMEONE'S WAITING FOR YOU," the innkeeper told Zora when she got there. "At the back of the restaurant."

A chill ran down Zora's spine with the dread that it would be Alegra, just to taunt her again. As she got into the corner of the restaurant, however, she saw Larzen. She turned to Natasha and told her to stay back.

"How did you find me?" Zora asked as she sat at the table.

"Why? Were you hiding from me? You do know you're breaching our agreement, right?"

Zora bit her lip. "I... didn't mean that."

"As to your question: I asked here and there. If you are trying to hide, this is quite useless. Everyone knows what you look like and it's not hard to notice you. Still, I shouldn't be chasing you, right? In theory, you should be available for me."

True. Zora then decided to tell him what had happened, starting with the horse and Alegra, then telling him about the assassin, the change of keys, and Alegra in her room. Of course, she didn't mention the princess and Griffin together. That was a key point, and it was weird to tell a story and omit its most significant part.

"And you went to Griffin for help? Why?"

Even Zora had no clue why she'd done it. "He asked me to tell him about anything related to security."

"He also asked you to quit the games."

"There's a difference."

Larzen tapped his finger on the table. "Listen here. I can see how he tried to be helpful, but my brother has been prepared for war. War is not subtle. It's blunt and crude. That's not how you deal with an assassination attempt, if that was really what it was."

"Oh, yeah, maybe the masked guy with the knife just wanted to say hi."

The prince chuckled. "I'm not saying that. It could have been someone sent to scare you. Someone who wants you out."

A horrible realization hit her. "Griffin."

"No, no, no. Of course not. My brother wouldn't do that. But it could be another champion, for example."

"And you don't think it could be Alegra?'

"The princess? No. She's too sweet for that."

Sweet. Right. If only he knew... But Zora just rolled her eyes. "Some poisons are sweet."

He leaned forward on the table. "You're not... jealous of her, are you?"

"Jealous as in wishing I were beautiful like her? Maybe. Jealous as in thinking I'd have a shot at something truly romantic with Kiran? No. I know my place, Larzen, please don't think I'm stupid. I have no delusions or feelings for the king."

"So stop thinking it's her, Zora. It's going to distract you from finding the true culprit. From what you described, she was concerned about you and that's why she got in your room.

It makes sense, right? She's a foreigner here. She'll obviously support the only champion she can identify with. A woman like her."

"I'm *not* like her."

"I meant you're both women. Of course you're not like Alegra."

Of course. It was obvious. And it shouldn't hurt. The memory of her and Griffin together hurt, though.

"Anyway," Larzen continued. "You need solutions and safety. I need you close and in the castle. I'll get you another room there. I promise I won't tell anyone, not any of my brothers, not Alegra. Still, if you keep guards following you, I can't guarantee the information won't spill. But that's up to you."

"I like the city."

"You can come here during the day, evening, when you're not busy. But our deal is to have you close."

"Can I bring Loretta?"

"If she wants. She'll probably get fed up with moving around, but it's up to you."

"All right." It's not as if she could say no, and in truth it wasn't as if she were that much safer outside the castle.

"Great. Now that this was solved, do you still remember you were participating in a competition? Cause see, as much as I would like to have warned you, I couldn't do that if I didn't know where you were."

"Sorry."

"That's not *my* problem, Zora."

"Let me guess. It's sword fighting."

"You got that right. And yet, you won't have time to learn anything."

Zora took a deep breath. "I thought about it. Learning is just a matter of effort. But unlearning is much harder. I can't undo an entire life of training in a specific style. So I don't think any training will help me."

Larzen was laughing. "Of course it won't. Are you serious? Who would learn anything in less than three hours?"

"What do you mean?"

He stared at her for a moment and tilted his head. "Zora, the challenge is this afternoon."

She caught a breath. It couldn't be. She wouldn't have enough time to prepare her potions, she wouldn't even have time to get mentally ready for a challenge.

ZORA WAS TREMBLING as she walked to the arena, Isabelle following her. She berated herself for having gotten so distracted that she lost her focus. But then, there was this thin suspicion that perhaps Natasha and Isabelle were told to get her mind off the competition, perhaps even make sure she didn't show up. Zora hated that feeling because until this morning she had considered the two girls her friends. And now she didn't know anymore. Natasha had claimed that she thought Zora knew about the challenge. It had sounded sincere, and yet...

Another thing that gnawed on her was the growing suspicion that Griffin had sent the assassin. It made total sense! How could someone enter the castle? Being authorized for it, of course. And then, Alegra with her key. Why, why had Zora ever thought that it could be only the princess, when she knew very well that she and Griffin were together?

Now, the worst part was that she had only done a very simple and not very effective speed potion, so her odds, which were already slim, were getting slimmer. Zora also missed Loretta's cheerfulness. Her friend wasn't at the inn when Zora took her things back to the castle, so all she did was leave a note to her friend.

Now Zora was staying in a room Larzen had given her, but she wasn't going to trust anyone anymore. She'd check the room when entering it, and bar it from the inside at all times.

But Zora had to forget all those thoughts, or she'd be for sure eliminated.

They entered the arena and Zora took her usual position, by Griffin. His bump was quite visible, and purple now. It was strange that he hadn't done anything to conceal it. And she didn't feel guilty about it anymore. He was right: he deserved it. But it was unfair. Any other person wouldn't manage to still look good with such a bump.

Only six competitors were left. Today only three would remain. They would all face each other with training swords. The goal was to touch the adversary with the sword or make them step out of a small circle on the floor. They weren't supposed to touch the opponents in any way other than with the sword.

Zora didn't feel she was prepared for that. At the same time, she was skilled with a sword, she knew it. The issue was how skilled her competitors were.

The first two to hit the circle were Klaus, the blond competitor from Gold Port, and Mauro. With his size, one would think that Mauro was all strength and no speed or skill, but that was not the case. He defeated his opponent quite easily, with fast, precise movements that got his sword on his opponent's chest a few times.

Then it was Griffin and a young, dark-skinned competitor from the Northern Pass. The prince was fast. Way too fast. The duel ended in less than ten seconds, as Griffin sent his opponent's sword flying away.

Zora had to face the tall young man with short black hair who had mocked her about slaying a lion. She'd even forgotten from where he was. He'd never done well in any challenge, and Zora was quite surprised he'd come so far.

As they stood against each other, he sneered and whispered, so that only she could hear, "Look at that. The prince's bitch. Question is whose. Maybe both?"

She'd better ignore him. If she got upset, she'd be falling into his trap and doing exactly what he wanted. Zora observed his stance, waiting for him to make the first move. They circled each other.

He then said, "All it takes to get the best horse is to ride a prince, right?"

Zora lunged forward. He blocked her and in a swift coup hit her arm.

She stepped back. This wasn't over. But she wondered for a brief second if that was what people thought of her. That brief second was too much. He hit her sword and somehow she blocked it, but then he moved his other arm towards her face and punched her. This wasn't part of the challenge. As she tried to recover from the surprise, she felt a boot on her ribs and was thrown on the ground. She rolled away before he lunged at her again. But he didn't attack her this time, now being held back by Griffin and Mauro. Zora sat. Her jaw and ribs hurt. She felt so stupid for having opened her guard so much. She could fight human shadow and would never let them get so close. What had happened to her?

Zora sat on the floor and watched as two guards took him away.

Griffin crouched in front of her. "He's been eliminated and arrested. How are you?"

He sounded concerned. Like always.

"Shocked," was all she managed to say.

"We can postpone the competition until you're better."

Zora glanced at the arena full of people. They would be angry if there was no challenge. And she would look weak. "This is nothing. I've fought shadow wolves while bleeding."

"This wasn't supposed to happen."

He was touching her face lightly and this was getting very awkward. She also dreaded the idea of anyone thinking that she and Griffin... Zora moved her head. "I'm fine." She pointed at him. "You're hurt, too."

He put his hand on his forehead and scoffed.

Zora swallowed. "We can go to the next round. I'm good."

The prince nodded.

The next fight was between the dark-skinned champion and Mauro. Mauro won.

Griffin took the blond competitor from Gold Port and again made his sword fly. It was odd how he was doing it so easily and so fast.

Then Zora was facing the prince and she realized that it hurt to move her arm because of her ribs. And he moved so fast. As much as she knew what he was going to do, somehow when his sword reached hers, she let it go. To make matters worse, she stumbled backwards and then found herself lying on the ground, the tip of his fake sword on her neck. Nice way to get back at her. He reached his hand to help her get up. She wanted to ignore it, but it would look really bad and rude in front of hundreds of people, so she took it. His palm was so soft. She pulled her hand as soon as she was up, and rubbed it on her pants, as if she could remove the feel of his hand in hers.

She had a duel right away, facing the blond competitor

from Gold Port. If he won, at least Loretta would be happy. Zora wasn't even sure if her friend was watching.

As she got to the center of the circle, it was hard to move, but she focused on blocking him. She did get a few light strikes on him, but he got a couple on her, too. A bell signaled that the duel was over. It had been a tie. That was an improvement.

Then the Golden Port and the Northern Pass competitor faced off each other. The blond guy got more hits and won. Good for Loretta.

Zora had to face the Northern Pass champion, then. If she lost, this would be over. She had to go back to the basics, to what she was good at, which was moving around, avoiding getting hit. They circled each other and she dodged him a couple times, but when she tried to attack him, he got his sword on her chest. She lost. That was it. She was going to be eliminated. Perhaps it wasn't the end of the world. But then she glanced at Griffin, staring at her, perhaps delighted that his plan had worked, or happy to get rid of her. She couldn't let it happen. If she lost, she wouldn't be able to face her parents, her students, her friends. But she'd better start getting ready for that, as losing as getting more and more likely.

The next adversaries were Griffin and Mauro. It looked as if it was going to be a balanced duel, proving that both of them were the best fighters there, but then Griffin did his signature move again. The ease with which he did it, there was something unnatural about it. Then she remembered his book, his suspicion about dark magic, him claiming that he knew about it... Of course. Griffin was the one cheating. Great.

Now Zora had to face Mauro. He was as big as or even bigger than a shadow human, but a lot more skilled with a sword. She didn't want to think about her odds.

15

A Picnic

Zora closed her eyes, trying to think. She had been doing it all wrong. Of course she didn't know how to block a sword, but she knew how to dodge sharp claws. She knew how to fight adversaries who were bigger than her. Perhaps all she had to do was imagine that Mauro was a human shadow and his sword was a claw.

They faced each other. His face had nothing of the friendly guy she knew, and she had expected no different. She was focused, too. When he lunged towards her, she saw the opening. He had his tall legs spread wide. Zora slid under them, turned, then jumped and hit his back. He fell forward, then she pressed her word against his back. A clear win.

"Did I hurt you?" she asked Mauro as they went back to their seats.

He shook his head, as if annoyed.

Only three competitors were going to move forward. She had one tie and one win, just like the blond competitor from Gold Port. Her heart beat fast.

As they announced the winners, Zora couldn't believe her

ears. She got third place, which meant she was still in. Beating Mauro, who had won almost all his duels, counted more points, and that was how she'd passed the competitor from Loretta's region.

Third place. She was doing worse at every challenge. This wasn't good. Still, she was in the competition, and that was what mattered.

When she got to her room, Larzen was waiting for her outside.

"We can talk there or in my office. What do you want?"

"Your office."

She followed him and entered a room with intricate golden chairs, delicate paintings of landscapes, and a huge hand-drawn map of Gravel and neighboring countries. Isabelle had followed Zora but remained outside.

"Here." He handed her an envelope. "I have this for you."

Zora sat down and opened it. It was from Loretta. Her handwriting was round with some flourishes. It was a goodbye note. She was leaving Gravel city to travel for some days. She had accepted Ephemerus's offer and wanted to spend some time with him. She also wished Zora good luck.

It felt like a punch in her stomach. Her only friend in this city. Gone.

"What is it?" he asked.

"She's leaving."

Larzen shrugged. "It's like that. People come with a goal, then when they reach it, they leave."

"I guess." She had something she wanted to tell the prince. "That champion who punched me, he insinuated that I'd been winning because I was sleeping with either you or Griffin. Is that what people think?"

"Think a little, Zora. Why would he say that?"

"To get me angry?"

He raised his eyebrows. "And I suppose it worked. I don't understand why people insist on offending women by suggesting they are free and do fun stuff, you know. They don't do that to men."

"How would he offend a guy?"

Larzen thought for a while. "Well, he could offend his sister, mother or wife."

"So it comes back to women." Zora rolled her eyes.

"I guess," Larzen said. "Or tell him he's a coward, he's not a man. Regardless, you need to understand why he probably hates you."

"Because I'm a woman?"

"Maybe. It's more likely he hates you because you've been doing well in every single challenge. Sour losers are sour losers."

"He should have focused on passing the challenge. Perhaps he could still be in the competition, if he didn't do something clearly against the rules and got himself eliminated. I'm wondering if someone paid him or something."

Larzen sighed. "Some people are guided by their emotions. You should pay them no mind. And stop being afraid of rumors. He'd probably tell you those things even if you had never spoken to any of us, just as a way to justify his inferiority. You're not going to quit my game, are you?"

"No." Zora had given it some thought. She wasn't afraid of making Alegra jealous, since it wasn't as if the princess could do any worse than try to kill her. And in fact, she'd welcome the chance to piss off Alegra and Griffin at the same time. "I understand what you mean now. The idea is to lay the trap instead of being trapped. Instead of being a potential target, a passive victim, I can play with his potential interest. You want me to seduce Kiran, right?"

"Sort of, I'd say."

Larzen was a bit clueless. Who in his right mind would notice Zora when he had Alegra? But she didn't want to be lectured on her need for self-confidence and yada yada.

Her question was a different one. "But what are you going to achieve with that? Even if we assume it's possible, he's not going to give up on Alegra, and she's not going to give up on him."

"Things are not as simple. It's about creating confusion. There are other pieces on the board. You can't judge the game based on a pawn's movement."

They didn't play board games in the Dark Valley, but she knew about them. "Pawns are sometimes sacrificed."

"True. But you won't, because you're smart. You're not a silly girl who'll fall for my brother's sweet words."

Zora stared at him. "If I were, you wouldn't care, would you?"

"If you were silly, you wouldn't be able to play this game. Like you said, you need to be in control to set the trap."

"I see. And what is the next step?"

He smirked. "As you know, there's no ball tonight. But we have a picnic tomorrow. Just for us, the family. You'll be my guest."

"Picnic?" It brought her bittersweet memories of the previous day and gave her an idea. "That sounds wonderful. Have you decided where to hold it?"

"By a lake, maybe."

"If you still haven't decided, would it be possible to have it by the mystic ruins? I went for a ride with my guards the other day and saw it from afar, but if we could get close..." She tried to sound sweet.

Larzen looked at her and thought for some moments. "Maybe. That could be interesting."

Zora smiled. "Thank you."

She could play games, too.

SOMEBODY DEFINITELY WANTED to stick a metaphorical knife in Griffin's gut. Larzen suggested the three brothers go out, like they used to do when they were younger. An opportunity for them to bond. The issue was facing Kiran. But he had to.

Other than that, he'd need to come back soon. So many things in his mind. An assassin within the castle walls. Zora's desperate shriek in his nightmares, echoing throughout the day. Alegra, he just wanted to keep away from her, and yet. And then the Blood Cup. He took a deep breath. No, that was easy. The last challenge proved that he'd have no issue defeating either Mauro or Zora, even if they were both talented in their own ways.

Griffin could see himself holding that cup—the key for his freedom. Then he'd never again fear for himself or what he would become.

When he met his brothers, his stomach churned. Alegra was accompanying Kiran, and Zora had been invited by Larzen. What did he even want with her? He'd need to talk to his brother, tell him to leave her alone. Either way, it meant an hour facing Alegra and Kiran. Perhaps it would be good and help him come to his senses.

A few guards stood at a distance, including one of the girls who had been appointed to protect the Dark Valley champion.

In the front were him, his brothers, Alegra, and Zora, who seemed recovered from her horse incident. She also looked recovered from the punch she'd received.

"So, where are we going?" Kiran asked.

"What about the mystic ruins?" Larzen suggested. "Zora and Alegra don't know it."

Yes. Someone definitely wanted to stick a knife and twist it.

They were looking at him and he shrugged. "I don't mind. It's an interesting place."

Could it be that one of his brothers had found out about him and Alegra? It couldn't be Kiran, or he wouldn't be so calm. Could Larzen have found out something? Or could it be that Alegra perhaps had planted the suggestion, as some form of cruel joke? The only thing to do was go and pretend not to be bothered by that place, even if he was guilty for what had happened between him and the princess, and worried about not remembering some parts of that day.

Larzen laid out a blanket on a different side of the ruins, not where he'd been with Alegra, which was some sort of relief. Perhaps this outing had not been planned to taunt him and was just a coincidence. Kiran was attentive to the princess. He probably liked her. Griffin felt awful.

Larzen... was more worried about the food than Zora. Perhaps he wasn't flirting with her. He'd better not. And her, he still had that agony in the very real feeling that something awful was about to happen. Griffin wished he could prevent it, but he had no idea how. At first he had thought that he needed her out of the competition, but then when she asked him not to kick her out of the games, with that "please" that wasn't quite as desperate as his vision, but still somewhat similar, it got him confused.

And he didn't know what to do other than try to find her

assailant, which seemed less and less likely each day. He'd also convinced her friend to leave the city. A friend who can't defend herself would be an easy target to hurt Zora. And yet none of that seemed to matter, as the feeling and the visions remained.

Fingers snapping in front of him brought his mind back to reality.

"What?" he asked.

Larzen laughed. "Griffin, what's the point in coming if you're not present?"

"I'm here."

"In body, only," Larzen said.

"Perhaps he's in love," Alegra suggested.

Griffin wanted to glare at her, but she didn't even deserve that. He shrugged. "It could be."

"You should have brought her, brother," Kiran said.

Griffin scoffed. "You're assuming she'd want to come."

"Weird." Larzen scratched his chin. "I thought that was what most girls wanted."

Alegra and Kiran laughed. Zora looked uncomfortable.

"Watch the language," Griffin warned Larzen. "There's a lady here."

"A lady? As in only one?" Kiran asked.

Griffin almost answered yes, which could have provoked his brother's ire, but then Zora said, "I'm not a lady."

Larzen stared at Zora. "I disagree."

Griffin didn't like his brother's tone or his stare. He shouldn't be flirting with the Dark Valley girl.

Zora looked away, not embarrassed, just as if avoiding being stared at.

Larzen looked back at Griffin and frowned. "You're sour,

brother. Are you going to tell us what happened to your forehead?"

Griffin touched his bump. "This? A lady did it."

Kiran laughed. "Griffin with a lady? That really deserves a celebration. I thought all you did was play with your sword."

"Gotta practice to get skilled." Griffin shrugged.

"Fact," Alegra said with a smile.

Griffin wished he could disappear.

"And is this lady beautiful?" Kiran asked.

Griffin glanced at Zora, who was glaring at him for some reason. He remembered her talent with objects. "Enchanting," he said between gritted teeth.

Color rose to Zora's cheek and then what had been a silly joke brought him some satisfaction and a smile. Perhaps just realizing that he affected her that way. She still glared at him, but there was something else there, too. And she *was* enchanting. Then suddenly his urge to keep her safe was taking a different tone, as if adding a new color to a landscape. Her bright eyes called him to her, the same eyes that looked even brighter with tears in his vision, eyes filled with pain and terror for something he still couldn't fathom. And the idea of seeing pain in her eyes crushed him.

"I want to see the ruins!" Alegra yelled, and then it broke the moment.

Griffin looked away. "I'll stay here." His mind was whirling. What had just happened?

They were debating who was going and who was staying, until he found himself alone on the blanket. Not for long, as Alegra walked back and smiled, "Changed my mind."

Griffin got up. "I'd better go."

"You make me sad. I'll wonder if you don't like the memory of us near here."

He shook his head. "Please don't wonder. Rest assured: I hate those memories."

She narrowed her eyes. "So ungrateful. Yet you were quite enthusiastic for someone doing something so horrible."

"I'm sorry. I'm sorry, Alegra. I can't do this."

She looked down, but instead of saying something, she started singing. Weird girl. He was turning to leave, then turned back. Alegra stood in front of him, more beautiful than ever. There was nobody else he wanted in the world, and he didn't care about his brother. Griffin rushed back to her and kissed her.

Alegra kissed him back, but pushed him after only a couple of seconds. "Not here," she whispered, still a little breathless. "Later. But there's a condition."

Waiting would be torture. "What condition?"

"Prove to me you don't like that girl."

He had no idea who she was talking about. "Who?"

"The champion."

"I have eyes just for you."

"Then humiliate her."

ENTERING ruins where dark and dangerous things could still spawn had taken a lot of courage. But perhaps it was true that anger and pettiness were great motivators. Zora wanted to piss off Alegra. And now she was here, with King Kiran, while Larzen had given her an excuse and gone back to join the others.

They were looking at a dungeon with mossy stones, rotting bars and some strange drawings forming triangles on a wall. "It must have been a castle, with these cells," Zora said.

"It might have been a temple. Some strange worshipping going on."

They stopped. She turned to him. "You know, I've given it some thought. I think I'd love to be your potion master, as long as I can return to my valley from time to time."

He smiled. "That sounds wonderful. We should start discussing the details soon."

It didn't sound bad. He wasn't being flirty at all and perhaps the whole thing had been one big misunderstanding.

Then he added, "Could you come to my room tonight?"

Zora laughed, then tried to sound playful. "You can't say that to a lady."

"I thought you weren't one."

"I was joking. Now, I know all you want is to discuss potions, but still. Sounds bad."

He looked around. "Nobody's listening. Come to my *office*, then. Does that sound better?"

"Much improved. But I'll be discussing this only after the games are over, not before."

He reached out a hand and ran a finger on her face. "It's bad form to make a king wait."

Zora jerked her head and turned around. "It is what it is. Let's go back."

She turned around and walked back to the meadow where the others were.

Griffin had stopped staring at her, which was a relief, but then he stared at Alegra a lot. Wasn't he afraid the others would notice?

When they were eating some cakes, Griffin said, "I have a question. This is supposed to be family time, and it explains why she's here." He pointed to Alegra. Then he pointed to Zora. "Why is she here?"

"I invited her," Larzen said.

"Are you inviting her to your bed, too?"

Zora wanted to throw something at Griffin again, but Larzen was faster and answered, "Unfortunately not." He sighed. "I wouldn't even try, frankly. This one here's as innocent as she looks. But she's nice to look at, isn't she?"

Griffin snorted. "That's a whole new take on nice."

Zora got up. "I'm here. I'm listening, and I'm leaving. I'm sorry that in this city people think everyone goes to bed with everyone. Maybe it's true, isn't it? What do you say? Griffin? Alegra?"

She turned around and ran towards her horse. Larzen was after her.

"I'm sorry. I don't know what's wrong with my brother."

Zora shook her head. "I can't stay. I'm tired of this. Tired of these so-called games, Larzen. I don't want to encourage an engaged man to flirt with me. It's disgusting. I don't want to do it anymore."

"This is not what we agreed."

"You said I could stop being your pawn and then you'd stop helping me. Well, stop it."

He tilted his head and narrowed his eyes. "I'll release Seth."

"I'll take my chances."

"Zora!" someone else called. Griffin was running towards them. Zora untied her horse as fast as she could.

Still, Griffin was there before she mounted it, that weird concerned look he had sometimes. "Is something wrong?" he asked.

"Everything is wonderful, Griffin." She didn't hide her sarcasm.

He frowned. "Are you all right?"

"I'm great. But I'm going back to the castle."

She rode towards the place where the guards were, tears running down her eyes. It was stupid to cry just because the prince was being rude, but she was tired of that. She was scared, too, about what would happen now that she had no more allies. None whatsoever.

Somebody wanted to kill her, and it could well be Alegra, Griffin, or them both, even if he sometimes pretended otherwise. She might have made things worse with her outburst. Seth would be out of prison and would certainly want revenge. On top of that, every day the Blood Cup seemed farther from reach. Natasha was riding after her, but Zora didn't really trust the girl anymore. And it hurt.

ZORA KEPT the room near Larzen's office, but he didn't call her again that afternoon. The next challenge would be the following afternoon, and it looked as if she'd have to go in blind. All she was going to do was prepare some very good potions for strength and speed and hope for the best. It was hard to concentrate, though, as at each and every moment she kept expecting guards to arrest her for impersonating a champion, or even Seth to knock on her door.

Sometimes she even wished one of those things happened, as the dread and anticipation were agonizing. On the other hand, she had made it to the semi-final challenge. Today they'd decide which two champions would battle for a chance at defeating the lion and getting the cup. She wasn't very positive about her odds of defeating Griffin. But thinking about it would be pointless. She had to focus on passing the current challenge first. Not that she'd spend any brainpower on it, since she had no clue what it would be.

In the hallway leading to the arena, Mauro was focused and distant, but Griffin approached her. "You ignored my summons."

True. She had received notes to see him, for more questions about her security. The issue was that she suspected him. But she wasn't going to confront him. "I... really? I must have forgotten."

"We'll discuss this later."

They entered the arena. Even though part of it was covered from their view, Zora saw three towers with some kind of golden cage on top.

The presenter explained the task: there were round boulders in the middle of the arena. The contestant who put the most boulders in their cage would win. The contestant with the least boulders would be eliminated. There were spiral stairs around the towers, which were high like some six floors or so.

Smooth, very smooth. The challenge was all about strength. And Zora was competing against two unnaturally strong men. Zora, whose strength was above average at best— for a girl.

Anyone going up those stairs carrying those boulders would have back pain for at least a week. Perhaps not Mauro. Maybe for him the boulders were just regular rocks, considering his size. Griffin... she still thought he had some dark magic, and perhaps it gave him unnatural strength. Zora had her strength potion, but yeah, it wasn't as if it could make her strength even close to those guys'.

She sighed as she felt the idea of holding the Blood Cup dissolving, as she dreaded going back to her valley and telling them she'd lost. They would blame her forever for having replaced Seth, for having taken that chance away from her valley.

The bell rang announcing the start of the challenge and she sat on the ground as she watched Griffin and Mauro running and grabbing a boulder each. She could run and try but it would be stupid. She doubted that she could even lift any of those boulders, let alone climb stairs with one. Perhaps if she could drag the boulders or chop them into pieces... But it would make her waste time, and wouldn't change the weight. She'd be chopping while Griffin and Mauro would be going up the stairs.

Zora had to think. She'd never win this challenge with her physical strength alone. Perhaps she'd never win this challenge period, so it was better not to struggle needlessly. She looked at the big cages.

An idea hit her.

Zora climbed her tower and checked if she could move the cage. No. Of course not. It had been attached to the floor of the tower using a lime-based cement. But it wasn't indestructible. Down there, in the arena, there were no tools. Zora took her sword.

"Sorry, Butterfly," she muttered.

It had been enchanted to be quite strong, but still... Zora had to try. She hit the base of the cage as fast and with as much strength as she could. She hit, hit, hit. Meanwhile, Griffin had two boulders and Mauro had three. At least if her friend won she would feel vindicated. Well, no. If she lost, Griffin would still go to the final and unless Mauro found some new, impressive trick, he'd lose to the prince. Zora kept hitting, while the minutes wasted away, her chances got smaller and smaller, and her sword got weaker and weaker. Perhaps this was foolish. When she felt that the base of the cage was weak enough, she pushed it. That took all her might. Push, push, push, then boom. It fell to the ground.

She ran down, aware that the time was almost over, then rolled as many boulders as she could into the cage, without even counting, without checking how many her adversaries had.

When the bell rang again, first she collapsed on the floor, her arms shaking from the effort of breaking down the cage. But she got up and stood beside Griffin and Mauro.

She wasn't crazy, the rules were to put the boulders in the cage, and she'd done it. That said... They could claim her method wasn't valid. Mauro was focused, looking ahead. Griffin looked at her with a satisfied smile. That couldn't be good. Oh, well, at least it would be known that she'd given her best.

16

THE POTION MASTER

The presenter stepped in front of them. "Oh, my, oh, my. Isn't this an unusual situation? I'm not even sure what to say." He approached Zora. "What do you say?"

"The rules were clear. Boulders in the cage." She pointed to hers. "They're there. Nobody said anything about where the cage should be."

The presenter nodded. "Valid points." He approached Mauro. "What's your opinion?"

"As a competitor, I'm neutral. I don't make the rules." He glanced at Zora with a certain apprehension in his eyes.

Then the presenter went to Griffin. "Your highness. Your opinion?"

"The Blood Cup tests a champion's strength, speed, and skills. In real life, in war, or in guard duties, we face challenges, too. And sometimes we need to find creative solutions. Zora's method is valid. Let the amount of boulders decide the winner."

This was strange. Had he said something against it, for example, that the boulders should have been put in the cage on top of the tower, not just in the cage, it would sway the public and she'd be eliminated. And considering how much he'd wanted her eliminated, including probably designing this challenge to be strength-based, it was strange that he wouldn't jump at the opportunity. Griffin was weird. Right now, it was something good.

The presenter consulted with some people, then the assistants came to count the boulders.

"The final results are here. Griffin: ten boulders. Mauro: eight."

Zora was surprised and disappointed. She'd been so sure her friend would beat the prince.

Then he continued, "Zora: twelve."

She was the winner! She was still in the games. She still had a shot. Tears came to her eyes with the relief that she wouldn't have to go home and explain why the valley didn't win. She could still do it! This had been close. So close. The very real fear of being eliminated, of losing, of having to come home empty-handed, made her realize how much she wanted this, how much she had to win. If she wanted to instill hope in her valley, she had to get that cup.

But before anything, she'd have to find a blacksmith to fix Butterfly and then redo its enchantments. Poor sword, so abused in this challenge.

THE BLACKSMITH LET Zora use his tools. Butterfly had some small bents that she was fixing.

Isabelle watched her. "You're good with this."

"What? Fixing a sword?" Zora shrugged. "Well, we have to."

"I thought you were going to break it in the challenge," the guard said.

"I feared that, too. But I had to give it a try. I'm glad it worked." Zora inspected her sword.

Isabelle laughed. "You won. That was so amazing. I didn't really get what you were trying to do, but then the cage fell with that thunderous bang, and I thought: yes, she has a chance. I'm glad they didn't say it was against the rules or something."

Butterfly seemed all right now. "So am I."

"Zora!" someone called her. It was Mauro, who ran in her direction. "What are you doing?"

She showed her sword. "Fixing the mess I made."

"We're going to the city to celebrate. Do you want to come?"

The two guys from Mauro's team stood back. Zora was wondering if he was asking it just to be polite or something. "Won't it be a problem?"

"Of course not!" Mauro sounded cheerful.

Zora turned to Isabelle. "Shall we?"

THEY WALKED to a tavern in Gravel city. It was so crowded, with people of all types, everyone drinking and making tons of noise. Mauro's friends were Sam, a thin young man with light brown hair, and Nando, an older, muscular man, who was the champion's trainer and mentor.

They got a pitcher of wine and five cups.

Isabelle shook her head. "I'm working."

Zora was considering telling her that it was all right, but if ever anything happened and they found out she had been drinking, she could get in trouble. She said, "I'm not drinking either. We can't in the Dark Valley."

"But you're not there! Just a little," Mauro insisted

"Half a cup," Zora said.

They toasted and she drank. It wasn't bad and certainly wasn't some dangerous poison. It tasted sweet and bitter at the same time, but in a way that made sense.

"Nice," she smiled. Then she looked at Mauro and his friends. "I'm so happy you invited me. Any other person would have been upset that they were eliminated."

"Ha. Are you confessing?" Mauro asked.

Zora stared at her cup. "Maybe. But I don't think I would be angry at you."

Mauro nodded. "That's the thing. Third place is a great honor. And at the end of the day, there isn't that much difference. It's not like any of us can beat the dark prince."

Zora frowned. "Dark prince?"

"It's his nickname."

She turned to Isabelle. "Is it?"

"We're not allowed to call him that. I think... people hear he likes dark magic. But he's a nice person, as far as I know."

"I'm not saying he's not nice," Mauro said. "I'm just saying we can't beat him, so it's not like I lost my chance at getting the bloody cup."

That made sense. Zora was thoughtful. "But why do you think that is? I mean, I can see why *I* can't beat him. But I don't understand why he beat you so easily."

Mauro laughed. "What are you saying? You beat me, crazy girl!"

"It was a one-in-a-hundred lucky move," Zora explained. "Our duel could have gone either way. Actually, you were much more likely than me to win. With Griffin... it was so quick. And he's much smaller than you."

"Size isn't everything." Mauro shrugged. "Which is sad news for me, or I would have won the cup."

Nando, Mauro's trainer, then spoke. "There's this idea that it's the royal line that gives the prince strength. Plus, he's been trained since he was little, by the very best the kingdom can afford. It's a mix of skill and determination. At least the skill is clear."

Zora crossed her arms. "Well, I've trained sword fighting since I was a baby."

Mauro spit his wine. "Baby? What can you even train at that age?"

The others laughed. Zora laughed, too, as the question hadn't been mean-spirited. "We give them toy swords and teach them some movements. It's play, but it's also training. Fine, serious training only once I could walk, of course."

"Like at two or so?" Mauro was still laughing.

"Well, yeah."

"And that might be why you're a finalist," Nando said. "Have you considered that? Now, you're small, too. Smaller and weaker than the prince. He probably had better teachers than you, no offense. So it makes sense he should win."

"It's a little unfair, if you think about it."

"I think he has the right to enter the games and prove his skills," Nando said.

He was very calm and rational. Zora wondered if Mauro had gotten his sayings from him. They went on talking about the Marshes and their farms. Mauro was happy with the payment for his participation in the games. He and Sam would renew their house. They gave Zora a paper with the name of the closest city and directions, in case she wanted to visit.

She felt a little sad that she couldn't really extend the same hospitality. Still, she tried. "Well, I'm in the Dark Valley, in the one village there is. If ever they allow visitors, you're welcome there, too."

"Perhaps they will. Gotta have a little hope," Marcus said.

Zora shook her head. "Hope."

SHE AND ISABELLE left when they were still celebrating and the tavern was still full. Despite the small amount of wine Zora had drunk, she had a pleasant, relaxing buzz, and understood why people liked to drink so much.

"They're so nice," Isabelle said about Mauro and his friends.

"They are."

As they walked back to the castle, Zora thought about Mauro and Sam, and their plans and hopes for the future. There was something beautiful in what two people could build together. A house was so much more than a house when it hosted people's love for each other. Even love for friends. She hoped one day she could indeed visit them. Love was powerful and beautiful, and yet, she still wondered if there would be a place for romantic love for her. Perhaps she didn't need it. Perhaps victory and hope could replace it.

"What are you thinking?" Isabelle asked.

"That I still want to win." She had to beat Griffin, there had to be a way.

"Oh, yes, you can't give up before it's over."

Zora turned to the guard. "But you don't think I have any chances."

Isabelle laughed. "What I think or not doesn't matter. What do *you* think?"

"I don't know." That was uncomfortable to admit.

They passed the guards at the gates and crossed the lawn and front gardens to the entrance of the residential area, where Zora was staying.

When they were getting close to the entrance door, Zora heard the sound of paws and saw three four-legged forms running after them. In a split second, she realized her sword wasn't strong enough to fight, and she wasn't going to take three animals at a time. She didn't know how well Isabelle could fight them.

"Climb!" Zora yelled as she jumped on a ledge on a window, then pushed herself up, so that she was far from whatever was coming.

Isabelle was struggling to climb. "I can't."

They were dogs, three angry, snarling dogs running at them. If they attacked Isabelle, Zora would need to jump down and help her. But they didn't, they ignored the guard. Instead, they were growling at the wall and trying to climb it. They were after Zora. Only Zora.

"What are those?"

"Quiet, quiet, calm down," Isabelle was telling the dogs, as if it would make them change their mind. She turned to Zora. "Prince Griffin's dogs."

Of course. "Why are they doing this?"

"I don't know!" the girl said. A dog turned to her, and she stepped back, saying, "Nice, nice doggie."

The ledge was very small and Zora had to use her arms for support. She feared she could fall. The dogs were jumping, trying to catch her, and if they jumped a little higher, they'd get her feet. Perhaps she should jump down and face them with her sword, as if they were shadow wolves, but Butterfly had lost its enchantments, Zora had drunk a little, and maybe wasn't as sharp as she should be. Plus, three at a time was a lot.

"Go get help," Zora told the guard. "Find someone. They seem to want to attack only me."

"Will you be all right?" Isabelle asked.

"As long as I don't fall! Hurry."

The girl walked backward, looking at the dogs, but they ignored her. When she was at some distance, she turned and ran.

"What's wrong with you?" Zora asked the dogs. "Taking after your lovely owner? Did someone send you after me? Grrrrr isn't an answer, you know?" One of the dogs jumped so high it was just a palm away from her foot. "Fine, it's a great answer. I'm not gonna argue with you guys."

Her hand was starting to hurt. And it was humiliating to be chased like that. And annoying that Griffin acted so nice in front of her, then turned around and did that. Well, actually, it made a lot of sense. Why would he confront publicly someone he wanted to kill? But then, sending his dogs, that was a little obvious. But then again, he was a prince. It wasn't as if he would be imprisoned.

Zora rested her forehead against the wall. There was nothing to do but wait.

AT LEAST TONIGHT there was no ball, just a small reception with some merchants. Griffin wanted to run, run far away. It was hard to face Kiran. At least Alegra wasn't there. His solace was that he would travel for sure once he won this competition. So close. His mind wandered while a man from the South Mountains talked. Hopefully Griffin was nodding on cue.

Then, from the corner of his eye, he saw a female guard at the door, pointing at him. Not any guard, one of the girls who had been assigned to watch Zora, her face worried. Griffin's nightmares and visions with Zora's desperate pleas came to his mind, with a horrible fear. He ran to the girl. "What's wrong?"

"Zora," she was breathless.

Griffin could feel his heart speeding up while his breathing stopped.

The girl continued, "The dogs are trying to attack her."

Trying. So it hadn't come to the worst yet. "I'll follow you. Let's run."

The girl ran and he followed her in the direction of the side walls of the castle. "What dogs?" he asked.

"Yours."

That didn't make any sense. Still, he kept running, then he saw a figure up on the wall, on a ledge, and dogs growling. He whistled—and they ran to him. It was indeed Wind, Snow, and Tempest. He patted their heads and was puzzled. They were normal. But they had been growling when he saw them.

He approached the wall. "Zora. They're calm now."

"Well, get them away from me. I don't want to decapitate any of them in self-defense."

"I'll put them in the kennel, where they should have been, but can you wait here? I need to talk to you."

"Whatever. Just get them away from me."

"Are you going to wait for me?"

"Yes," she yelled.

Griffin led the dogs to their kennel. There was no sign that it had been forced open or anything, and he didn't understand why they were outside. Still, even if someone let them lose, why would they attack Zora? It didn't make sense.

When he got back to the lawn surrounding the castle, Zora was there, arms crossed. "Can we go to my office?" he asked.

"Why? So you'll kill me?"

He wasn't sure if she was joking. "Kill you?" He pointed at the guard. "In front of a witness?"

"As if her word counted anything against yours." Zora sounded angry.

Griffin must have misheard something, it wasn't possible. "You think I'm a murderer? And I want to kill you?"

"Explain the dogs."

"I can't. And I won't be able to, unless you explain what's happening."

"Fine. Let's talk."

She followed him to his office in silence, her guard trailing behind them. He had a key now, unsure about the efficiency of his magical lock after the knife had disappeared.

Her guard, Isabelle, remained in the hallway.

Once the door was closed, before he even had time to seat, Zora said, "I know why you want me dead."

"You do? Enlighten me."

"That's not funny," she said.

For some reason he started laughing. "I'm not saying it's funny."

She glared at him and the laughter died.

Zora took a deep breath, as if gathering courage to say what she was going to say. "It's not my fault I saw what I saw. I'm sorry. Now just think a little. Why would I get entangled in a mess I have no stake on? For which I have no proof? I have no intention of telling anyone. First, I'd gain nothing with it. Second, it would be stupid. So just leave me be."

"You saw..." Realization hit him. "You saw me... and..." He couldn't even say her name, admit it aloud. He stared at the floor. "I have no words, no excuses, nothing. You must think I'm despicable."

"I don't think anything," she yelled. "I'm not engaged to anyone. I don't care. I don't want to tell anyone anything. Stop trying to kill me."

"I'm not trying to kill you, Zora. I was at a reception tonight. The entire night. I wouldn't have had time to set my dogs loose. Even if I had, I wouldn't know how to make them go after you. And I would have no reason for that."

She stepped back. "Keeping your secret is a good reason."

"If I keep being careless the way I've been, the secret will be out soon. Why would I kill anyone?"

"Because someone attacked me, then your dogs attacked me."

"And I did everything I could to find the culprit, didn't I?" he asked.

"I don't know. Alegra has two attendants. Did you check any of them?"

Of course he had, that was the first thing that came to his mind, even if he didn't think Alegra had done it. But he didn't remember it clearly. He then felt a sharp jolt of pain on his head and put his hands on it.

"Griffin?" Her voice was laced with worry. "What's happening?"

"Headache," he managed to say. Then he sat down and took a deep breath.

"Do you want me to call anyone? Give you something?"

The pain was gone. "No. I'm fine." His mind was fuzzy, though. "What were we talking about?"

She frowned. "Were you pretending?"

"No. I... sometimes I forget things."

"Then maybe you set your dogs on me and forgot it."

That was what they had been talking about. His dogs. Someone trying to kill her. There was something else... Could he have set his dogs? "I was at the reception. I can ask someone if I left."

Zora rolled her eyes and shook her head. "Just tell me. What can I do for you to stop trying to kill me?"

"It's not me." How could she even think that?

"Then it's Alegra. But you're not going to check her or her attendants, are you?"

"I think... I checked?"

"You think. That's amazing." Her anger was clear.

He tried to explain himself. "It's not me. I'll keep trying to find out who it is. Meanwhile, be careful."

"I am careful, but I'm not invincible."

There was something else he wanted to mention. Something that had been bothering him. "Zora, I was rude to you at the picnic. I... don't remember what I said. Whatever it was, I'm sorry."

"Is that your excuse? That you don't remember things?"

"Yes. I know it's terrible." He knew how bad it sounded.

"You're right."

He took a deep breath and decided to tell her what had been bothering him. "Do you believe in visions? Premonitions?"

She looked surprised, perhaps with the change in subject. "I don't know. Some people in our valley are superstitious, but I'm not."

Griffin looked at her. "It sounds strange, but I had a vision about you. Just you, in distress, something horrible happening. It's been in my mind ever since."

She stared at him for a while, probably thinking he was weird or worse, was lying. "A vision?"

218

"Be careful," he said. "And understand that I want no harm to come to you. Those visions disturb me. I just want you to stay safe."

"While at the same time defending Alegra, who might be trying to kill me. Makes total sense. Well, actually, considering how *close* you are, it does make sense."

Could it be that she knew about them? "What do you mean?"

She raised her hands, as if in defeat. "I give up."

"Tell me."

She rolled her eyes. "I'll repeat, since you're all forgetful. I know about you two, and I think that's why either you, her, or both of you are trying to kill me."

Pain, so much pain, as if his head were being crushed under a boulder.

Her voice came from far away. "Amazing acting. Congratulations."

Zora was almost falling for his scene again, especially now that his face contorted in pain and he fell on the ground. She had to fight every instinct not to rush to him and try to help, but she opened the door and left. Isabelle wasn't alone in the hallway. Kiran stood by her. "So, who did you see?"

Her heart skipped a beat.

Kiran walked her to his office. Once they were in, he said, "Soundproof. Unlike Griffin's. Now tell your king who you saw, and where."

Zora's mind had been spinning trying to find an excuse. She didn't want to be the one to reveal such a thing. "I'm not sure. It was a guess. I think Princess Alegra wants to kill me, and I thought... But it's an assumption."

He crossed his arms. "When did you see them?"

"In the picnic. The way they looked at each other. I think he's attracted to her, that's all. Can't blame him, she's gorgeous, but I don't think—"

"Will you stop babbling? You were very certain while talking to him just now." Kiran sounded angry.

"I wanted him to confess, in case he was the one trying to kill me."

"And why do you think he'd want you dead?"

"Because someone's trying to kill me."

Kiran took a deep breath. "I'm going to try to explain something to you. Me and Alegra, it's just appearance, so people think I'm seriously considering a queen. She plays her part well. We're not romantically involved. I don't care if she's seeing my brother. Yes, I wish they had told me, but on the other hand, perhaps it would have been awkward. But if I know it, it changes things. Goodness, we need an alliance with Linaria, it can be with Griffin, though. If that's the case, the solution is easy."

Zora wasn't sure she believed him, but he was calm and sounded sincere. "I see. But I don't know much. I'm assuming."

"Just tell me what you're assuming. Weren't you going to be my potion master? Let me know I can trust you."

Perhaps it was better to say the truth. "I visited the Mystic ruins one day before the sword challenge. Alegra and Griffin were there. I saw their horses."

"Alegra doesn't have a horse, and that day, my brother had a horse from the stable. How did you know it was them?"

"I heard them talking."

"So you eavesdropped."

"No, I just heard their voices and walked away."

"You're not telling me everything, Zora. I can have your guards interrogated, or your friend interrogated, even if she's already far from here. Tell me what you saw."

Zora exhaled. "I saw their clothes. Alegra wears a specific type of embroidery, and Griffin wears that same vest all the time. I walked away when I saw that."

He looked at her for a moment and smiled. "Was it that hard to say?"

"Yes, because I can't be totally sure it was them, and..."

"Why didn't you come to me earlier?"

"I wasn't sure. And maybe you wouldn't believe me. I'm sorry."

He shook his head. "It's fine." Then he chuckled. "Griffin. Who could have guessed? Would you pick him?"

"It's not my place to pick any of the royal highnesses." She didn't even know if she was saying it right.

He chuckled again. "Of course. Go to sleep, it's late. Tomorrow I'd like to talk to you about your appointment and the Blood Cup. I'm pretty sure we'll find a nice agreement."

"What are you going to do about... what I just told you?"

"I'll wait until the games are over. It's only two nights away. Then I'll talk to both of them." He shrugged. "For me it's a relief, frankly."

"I'm glad it's the case. But... someone is trying to kill me, and I think it could be Alegra. Or even Griffin. If they knew it wasn't a big deal..."

"I'll keep an eye on them, don't worry. For now, just keep being careful, and you should be fine."

It wasn't a good plan. Still, she said, "Thank you."

Zora got out of his office and headed to her room, Isabelle walking by her. She actually had to resist the urge to go check if Griffin was feeling better or if he was sick or something for real. No, it was a pretense. And it would look odd to go knocking on his door out of nowhere, especially after what she'd just done.

Her talk to Kiran gave her a dreadful feeling, but she had to trust that he wouldn't want to harm his brother and had to trust the calm with which he received the information.

Once inside Zora's room, Isabelle asked, "What happened?"

"Nothing. The king wants me as his potion master, that's all."

Isabelle had an odd look. "Is that something you want?"

"I just want to win the cup and stay alive meanwhile," Zora confessed. "Is it true you're not reporting to anyone what I'm doing?"

"It is. Don't worry. I'm not telling anyone what happened, unless you want me to."

"Don't say anything. People can come to wrong conclusions."

"I don't plan to."

Zora had another curiosity. "Did you hear what I was talking to Griffin?"

Isabelle shifted as if uncomfortable, then said, "No. There's a special way to listen inside. I saw the king doing it but I wouldn't do it. "

That made things slightly better, if it had been only Kiran.

Zora then set up her enchantment table. She wasn't sure the girl wouldn't tell anyone she'd spoken to Kiran, and she could only guess what they would think if they learned she went straight to the king after talking to Griffin.

All she could do for now was make sure she had a fast, precise, and strong sword, which she would carry with her at all times. Then she would make some more potions. Two days. She could do it. And perhaps she would even find a way to win. Then there was the matter of the lion. Yes, she had killed shadow wolves, but she'd been desperate and had been sure she'd die. A lion would be huge, very strong, and not something she was used to fighting against. But then, she had to defeat the prince first. One thing at a time.

17

THE FINAL CHALLENGE

Zora exercised in a garden in the castle. This time she
hadn't asked Natasha to spar with her, so the guard only
watched at a distance.

She did her regular Dark Valley forms with a practice
sword, which was likely what they would use for the last challenge. They had movements for attacking, dodging, that they
practiced so much they got ingrained in them. When it was
time for combat, there was no need to think about what to do.
But the instinct only came after a lot of repetition. And that
was what she was doing. She had to trust the knowledge she
had, had to see Griffin and his sword as if it were a human
shadow and its sharp claws, had to dodge and avoid him until
she found an opening.

She had a chance and had to believe it.

Someone stood at the edge of the patch. Larzen. Zora ran
to him, as she felt guilty that she'd stopped helping him.

"I haven't heard from you," she said. "I'm sorry. I think I
was ungrateful."

Larzen tilted his head, as if pointing at Natasha. "Won't she hear us?"

"She's far." But Zora spoke at a lower volume. Then she looked at him. "You didn't release Seth." She felt guilty about that, too.

"Actually, I did. I put him back in the Dark Valley, warning him that if he escaped again, he'd be imprisoned for life."

"You didn't tell me."

"No, because I wanted to use him as leverage. Thing is, it's not that easy to keep a prisoner a secret."

"And he was fine? He didn't try to do anything?"

"He was sedated all the time. I don't know what he'll do in your valley, though. He probably won't be happy about you."

Zora looked down. "I'll deal with that." She'd have to face him, but in a way, she'd even welcome the chance to confront him. She looked up and faced the prince. "Is there anything you need from me now?"

He shook his head. "I miscalculated. It didn't go the way I thought it would."

Zora wanted to ask which way that was, but then thought he'd probably not want to tell her. If he really thought the king could get interested in her, he was worse in the head than Griffin.

Larzen continued, "And plus you know what the next two challenges are going to be. Unfortunately, I have no tips to help you beat my brother."

There was a certain sadness in his voice. Zora wished she could do something. "Is there any problem? Anything I can do? I don't mean as part of some deal, but..."

"I..." He took a deep breath. "Should have seen certain things much earlier."

So enigmatic. Zora laughed. "You're going to leave me here dying with curiosity?"

He chuckled. "I doubt you'll be curious for long."

"Right. You definitely want to kill me."

Larzen looked at her for a while, then said, "I'll give you one clue. It has to do with Griffin."

Her insides churned. Did Larzen also know about his brother and Alegra? And what did it have to do with Zora? Unless the whole thing had something to do with splitting the Linaria princess and Kiran. In this case, there was no need to do anything anymore. She still felt an emptiness in her stomach, fearing some retaliation against Griffin.

"I hope it's nothing bad," she said.

He smiled. "I think it's something good, but it's up to you to decide."

That didn't make sense and she didn't want to get any more involved than she already was. "Well, I'm not interested in any brother business or anything. I'm sorry I asked. I'll find out when it's time to find out."

Larzen nodded. "Wise. Everything in its time. Any clue on who's trying to kill you?"

Yes, but she didn't want to discuss it with even more people. And perhaps his question meant he was unaware about Zora having seen anything. She shook her head. "Not really."

"Be careful, then."

Be careful, be careful. It was all people told her. As if the responsibility for not getting murdered were hers.

Zora had been called to Kiran's office, and she hoped he didn't want to ask her more questions or perhaps even confront her. To her surprise, he was in a good mood, and smiled when he saw her.

"How can I help your majesty?" she asked.

"Phew majesty." He waved a hand. "Do you have a plan to defeat my brother?"

"Fight the best I can." She shrugged.

"Do you think it's enough?"

"Probably not."

He gestured to a chair. "Sit, sit. I have a suggestion. And it might be a test, too. About your skill with potions."

Zora didn't think that even the best strength and speed potions would be enough to beat Griffin. It would be awful if the king thought that could be the case. Still, she just asked, "What's your suggestion?"

"It's an offer. If you make a potion for confusion, I don't know, slowness or something, I can give it to him."

A cold dread came to her. This would be cheating. And quite shameful. "I don't think it's allowed."

"Nonsense. The competition tests skill and smarts, too. Sometimes you have to improvise and be creative, don't you think?"

Zora was wondering if she could even make a potion like that. Perhaps it was a nasty thing to do, but Griffin wasn't being honest either, with his weird dark magic or something, and plus he was either trying to kill her or enabling someone who was. "I guess. I could do that. But why would you help me win?"

His hazel eyes sparkled. "Oh, you know I like poetry and art. And beauty. You do realize you're nicer to look at then my brother, right?"

"But I can be looked at without having to win..."

He laughed. "Never underestimate a king's desire to inspire

loyalty." He stared at her. "Remember I want you." That was uncomfortable. Then he added, "As my potion master." It didn't improve much.

He continued, "Plus, it's just a cup. Griffin doesn't need it. You on the other hand, would be different. It would be poetic. Inspiring. The least likely champion ends up winning. It's a lot more entertaining, isn't it?"

It didn't really make sense for him to want a commoner besting a royal, but it sure could be entertaining and inspiring, even if not in the way he was thinking. "I guess."

She paused, considering. This decision was one she would not be able to come back from. But she had to win. After she won, she could make an excuse and not be his potion master or whatever else he wanted from her, or maybe he'd eventually ignore her.

Zora took a deep breath. "I'll brew a potion. But there's an issue of timing. Something like that would have a short effect, and I don't think you can reach him right before he enters and say, 'Here, drink a potion!' you know?"

"Would the effect be that immediate?"

All the information about potion-making was circling in her head. "Actually, it takes about five minutes to ten minutes."

"Is there a way to delay it?"

She could make it in such a way that it would take longer to take effect. Complicated but feasible. "I could delay it to half an hour. There's also an issue of taste."

"What if I mixed it with grape juice or something?"

Her heart was beating fast. She knew it as wrong, but at the same time, sometimes only one wrong could fix another. "It would work."

"Tomorrow then, before the challenge, we'll have a champions toast. What time can you get this potion ready?"

This would be the most difficult potion Zora had ever brewed. "Late afternoon."

"It needs to be earlier. The competition will be at three. My brother insisted it couldn't be at night."

The time was tight, but she could try to hurry. "I'll give it to you at two."

He smiled. "That works, and I'll make sure he drinks it."

"Thank you so much. That's very kind."

"You know it's not kindness. It's strategy." He shrugged. "It makes more sense for you to win, that's all."

"I'll be here tomorrow with the potion."

Zora walked away with hope that she could win this challenge, some guilt for cheating like that, and a slight dread of later having to face a lion. Yes, she had defeated shadow wolves before, but it hadn't exactly been easy, and she could have died. She'd need to put her life at risk again if she were to face an animal as huge as that. But then, she had to win, and if the price was her life, so be it. The moment she had stolen that rod and written her name on that letter, she had sealed her destiny, so she'd better make the best of it.

The potion took a lot of thought. She had to think about ingredients with opposite properties. It was a good thing that she hadn't only memorized potions, but understood their composition. That way she could do a reverse-speed potion and a reverse-alertness. She figured she could also add ingredients to reduce his strength, but then the taste would be too strong. And a sword duel wasn't really about strength, but about speed and reflexes. She also did a speed potion for herself, just in case. And she made sure to get enough sleep, otherwise she would be dooming her own alertness.

There was always the small risk that Kiran wouldn't have an opportunity to give the potion. And maybe the potion wouldn't work that well on Griffin if he had some other magic. But Zora was going to try her best and fight until the end.

THEY HAD SET up tables in the area behind the arena. Kiran and Griffin were there, together with a few guests.

"I propose a toast for our finalists!" Kiran said, then filled cups with wine.

Griffin took the wine! No. He was supposed to refuse it and take the grape juice. Zora took the wine, too, but she was going to take just a sip.

"Any words to your adversary?" Kiran asked.

"Good luck," Zora said to Griffin.

He smiled. "Same to you."

"Oh, that's boring," Kiran said. "I'm sure you can find more interesting words than that."

"I have to focus," Zora said. "I can't come up with pretty words."

"It's been an honor," Griffin said. "And whatever happens in the arena, it will still be an honor."

"Thanks." Zora tried to smile. She felt embarrassed and also worried because he wasn't drinking the juice. Her plan was flopping.

She looked around and felt that something was amiss. Well, yes. Larzen wasn't there. Perhaps he didn't care anymore now that his game was over or something. The Linaria princess wasn't there either, but that made sense. She wasn't going to continue posing as Kiran's betrothed, and it would be too early to show up with Griffin.

Zora took a glass to get some water.

Griffin stood by her. "There's juice, too."

"I prefer water. You're drinking? So confident that you don't even mind fighting me while tipsy?"

"I'm not gonna get tipsy with half a cup of wine. But yes, I could still fight you after a couple cups."

What an asshole. "Oh, yes. Puking is quite a surprise move."

He laughed. "Don't worry. I'll switch to juice."

Griffin put his cup on the table and took another cup. Zora looked away, afraid that he'd notice her interest in what he was drinking or whether he was pouring the juice.

He extended his hand with his cup. "So. Shall we do a non-alcoholic toast? Champions only?"

Sure. She raised her cup with water. He raised his cup with the juice and drank it all. Zora glanced at Kiran, who glanced at a clock. So the challenge would be half an hour from then. She felt as if there was a chilly breeze inside her stomach. Perhaps it was a mix of fear, apprehension, and even a little guilt. Then perhaps it was an odd anticipation of seeing her goal so close. And yet, there was that fear that something could go wrong. She could even feel her heart beating fast. This wasn't good. She'd need to sit by herself for some time and breathe slowly. She needed to be ready in case the potion didn't work as well as she expected, and ready to defeat the youngest prince. The dark prince.

Zora sat down, hoping those people would go away and let her focus. King Kiran approached her. "There's a spectacle before the challenge. I'd like you to sit by my side to watch it."

"I need to get ready. Mentally."

"You can do it at the royal box. Come." He offered her his arm.

It was very strange to sit by the king, at the place that had once been Alegra's. She didn't even want to imagine what people would start to say about her. The royal box was on a platform near the ground, but with a roof above it and glass between it and the arena.

The jugglers and acrobats entered for their performances, but she couldn't enjoy them as much. All she felt was the time passing. Twenty, twenty five minutes. If they took too long, the effect of Griffin's potion would wear off. And her odds would be greatly reduced. She also didn't understand why Kiran wanted her in the royal box.

"Where's Griffin?" she asked.

"Getting ready."

"I need to get ready, too."

"There's time." Kiran didn't seem worried.

Well, he was unlikely to care that much about who won and who didn't.

The jugglers soon walked away from the arena. Griffin's potion should be taking effect right now, and she hoped she could go down there and face him while he was confused and slow, if ever her potion worked.

"I need to go," Zora pleaded.

"No, no. You won't want to miss this."

Kiran didn't get it.

Someone pushed the lion cage to the center of the arena. Right. They wanted to remind everyone what the winner would face. Yikes. As it became closer to reality, Zora felt she was getting more sorry for herself than the lion, which was roaring and walking around in its cage in a menacing stance. It would still be sad to kill him. But being killed by him would be even sadder.

The cage had a strange closing mechanism attached to a rope, and a man took its tip and walked away from the arena. Her heart started beating fast. Would they move straight to the final challenge? She wasn't ready. "What's happening?"

"A spectacle, my dear." He laced his hand on hers, which was very weird and embarrassing, in case anyone saw it and came to inappropriate conclusions.

Griffin walked into the arena, carrying a lance and a shield. Zora felt as if her heart stopped. They would make him face the lion? In that state? Zora would become a murderer. The entire audience in the arena would witness a gruesome spectacle. A spectacle which would be all Zora's fault. She looked again, as if to check she wasn't mistaken, and to check Griffin. His eyes were unfocused, distant, as if... As if he'd taken a potion to block his reflexes. She pulled her hand and turned to Kiran.

"You have to stop it," she pleaded. Tears were running from her eyes.

He laughed. Laughed. It was his brother. How could Kiran do that?

"Please!" Her plea became a shriek as she noticed the man pulling the rope.

No. Zora wasn't going to become a murderer. She took her sword and hit the glass, which shattered, then, before she knew what she was doing, she had jumped into the arena and was standing before an enormous lion running towards her. She needed the lance and shield, but had no time to turn to take them from Griffin, so she threw Butterfly, turned, took Griffin's weapons, then turned again and saw the lion almost on top of her, but managed to poke the animal with the lance. The lance broke, though, and all she had was the shield and her sword, which was now far away, behind the lion.

"Behind me," she said to Griffin, hoping he could at least do that.

"I'm... not..." he mumbled.

"I know." The potion had been too strong.

She managed to keep the lion away with her half lance, and circled it. She had to get to Butterfly. As short as it was, at least it was sharp and fast, it was the sword that she trusted, with which she had defeated shadow wolves. When she reached it, she threw the lance at the lion, then the shield. Let it come to her. The way she'd always trained.

The animal lunged towards her, and she swung her sword and cut part of his neck at the right time. Had it been smaller, it would have been beheaded. The animal fell on top of her, one of his claws cutting her arm.

Horrified, covered with blood, Zora crawled from under the corpse—and saw Griffin fallen behind her. The potion had been way too strong. She hadn't completely evaded being a murderer. Zora checked his pulse and exhaled in relief when she noticed he was still alive.

She was going to ask for help, when she heard Kiran's booming voice. "Arrest her. Kill him."

What? She was encircled by armed guards, but they approached cautiously, perhaps even with some hesitation.

"He's your prince! Don't hurt him," she pleaded.

She realized she was a pathetic sight, sobbing over his unconscious body, as if trying to shield him.

"Anyone who disobeys me will be sentenced to death," Kiran yelled. "Kill him. And her, if you have to."

It was all Zora's fault. There was no way she could face all these guards. There were also archers on the top benches. An arrow flew above her. Well, she wasn't going to die like a coward. Zora stood up, Butterfly in hand. An arrow hit her shoulder. What a sad way to die.

Zora then heard someone singing. The guards all stopped.

Everyone stopped to look at the red-haired woman walking onto the arena. Alegra. What was she doing there?

"Run. Get him away from here," the princess muttered, before continuing singing.

She was enchanting them somehow. And helping Zora. Or rather, Griffin. Zora then noticed that the princess wasn't wearing any of her pretty dresses. Instead, she had an ugly burlap thing covering her. And managed to look magnificent with it.

Zora had better take her chance and get the prince away from there. She tried dragging him, but he was so heavy. She had no clue how to take him to safety, no clue how long Alegra could hold everyone off.

Two figures stepped in the arena. Mauro and Sam.

"I'll carry him," Mauro said while picking up Griffin. "Follow me."

He led her out of the arena and to an area with horses. The attendants who should be tending the horses and carriages were also frozen in place. Mauro put Griffin on the back of an empty cargo cart, with horses still attached to it, and turned to Zora. "It's ours. Take it and get away from here."

"I don't know how to... control this thing."

Mauro jumped on the front. "I'll take you out of the city, and you'll learn on the way." He turned to Sam. "I'll be right back."

"Wait," Sam said. He took off the cloak he was wearing and handed it to Zora. "To cover the blood."

"Thanks."

They moved away from the castle, not very fast, as that thing had only one horse. Hopefully Kiran would take long to realize where she'd gone.

"What happened? Why did they change the challenge?" Mauro asked.

"I... don't know." She looked down.

"You were quick to notice that the prince had been poisoned."

Poisoned. That was the right word. Zora swallowed. "Yeah. I... Started to notice adversaries. Stuff."

"That princess saved you."

"*You* are saving us." She had a curiosity. "How come you weren't affected by her strange singing?"

"Might be something love or lust based. My heart's already taken."

Zora shrugged. "Well, I have a hole where mine should be."

"But she didn't want to control you."

"Makes sense." She looked down, then back at her friend. "I have no words to thank you."

"No need to. You're right that he's our prince. And you're my friend. You were brave today."

"You're being brave, too."

"No, Zora. If I were brave I would have jumped in that arena. I didn't. I didn't even consider it or understood what was happening until he collapsed and you killed the lion. That's the problem with people, they won't jump into danger to defend what's right."

"Why should they? They have nothing to do with it."

Mauro pointed at her. "You did."

If only he knew the reason why she had jumped, the reason why she had known Griffin wasn't in a fit state to face the lion... Perhaps he'd hate her. "How do I give you back this cart?"

"Don't worry about it. Now pay attention. This is much like riding, what you do with the reins. Can you try them?"

Zora took them and followed his directions. It wasn't too bad. Hopefully she'd manage it.

They weren't yet outside the city when he jumped out. Zora remembered the way to the Dark Valley. Sort of. She remembered the street she took to come into the city. It was the only place she could think of going. Her parents would help her with her wounds. Her shoulder was bad and her arms were bleeding. She would help Griffin, too, if the potion had caused him to get sick. Still, she dreaded the idea of having to confess what she'd done. Everything she'd done.

18

REVELATIONS

After travelling for some time, when she was away from the city, on a quiet road, she stopped to check on Griffin. The prince was still breathing, but his face was pale and his pulse was slow. Improvising a potion had been such a stupid idea. Now his life was at risk. Because of her. She couldn't go to the front and leave him in this state.

"Griffin. Griffin." Perhaps he could wake up, perhaps she could make sure he stayed alive. It was better for him not to be unconscious. She felt as if his life was fading from him, and tried again. "Griffin. Please wake up. Please stay in this world. Please don't die."

Tears were running from her eyes again. If they could fix anything, Zora would have no problems.

"Please," she pleaded again.

Well, pleading wasn't going to help if he was really unconscious.

Griffin exhaled. "Zora?" He sounded relieved, just like that time when he'd been drunk. As if he was happy it was her.

"Yes."

He took her hand and sat up.

"Don't..."

He shook his head. "I'm fine."

More tears were forming in her eyes, this time tears of relief. "Really?"

He looked at her, as if surprised. "It was you. That night. It was you." He frowned, as if thoughtful. "Your desperation... was for me?"

"Not desperation, I just..." She didn't even know what to say. The truth would be horrible.

"You jumped in front of a lion, Zora? For me?" He looked so surprised and hopeful. There was even some misplaced admiration in his look.

Zora was embarrassed. "I saw you... were... I don't know. Confused?"

His hand was still holding hers and she thought it was getting sweaty and sticky, and it was warm, but she didn't want to pull it.

Griffin then ran his other hand through her hair. "You really care."

That was confusing. Even more confusing when his lips touched hers, softly, slowly, as if inviting, as if asking. What was her answer? Her answer was obviously no, but her mouth had a different opinion, as she kissed him back. Her hands had a different opinion, too, as they were caressing his hair, that soft hair, that feel she'd never forgotten.

He let go of her hand and had his arms around her. The strong arms she once thought were stupid, the arms she'd always wanted right there where they were. She was kissing Griffin. Kissing him back. And she realized that on a scale from "it would be nice if" to "I'd love this", kissing him had its own special category, a desperate need she couldn't quite put into words.

But then reality hit her, the fact that he loved someone else, the fact that he was a prince and she was nobody, the fact that she had betrayed him. She pushed him away. "We can't do this."

"Why?"

She crossed her arms. "I'm not Alegra, for one."

"I don't care about her. Not anymore."

"Maybe. Maybe you're lying or deceiving yourself. Plus you're a prince and... I'm not. You'd want just one thing."

"That's not true." He frowned as if confused. "Why did you kiss me back?"

She looked away and shrugged, as if she didn't care. "It was a good kiss."

He was silent for long seconds, then said, "I'm sorry, then. For kissing you. I thought... I was wrong." Griffin lay down and closed his eyes.

Zora touched his shoulder. "You're not gonna die, are you?"

He looked at her. "Oh, what do you care?"

"It was a lot of hassle to keep you alive, Griffin, and I don't like it when people ruin something I put effort in."

"I'm not dying." He sat up again and looked around. "Where are we going?"

"The Dark Valley. You might need help. I need help, too." She pointed to her shoulder. "An arrow hit me."

"You'd better clean it."

"If I find a river. I just thought of the Dark Valley because it's close. It's less than a day away. But if you have a better suggestion..."

"Why are we leaving Gravel city?"

Zora looked down. It was hard to say that. "Your..." She took a deep breath. "Brother. Told the guards to... kill you."

"How did you escape?"

"Some people helped me." She should tell him about Alegra, tell him that perhaps the princess still loved him, but a selfish part of her didn't want to tell him that.

He was thoughtful. "The Dark Valley is close. But it's heavily guarded. And it will be the first place they'll look for us. Are they after you, too?"

"I'm under arrest orders only. They'll kill me only if necessary."

Anger flashed in his eyes. "My brother ordered you killed?"

"Arrested. Because I was defending you."

"He had no right." He thought for a moment. "News travels slowly. Maybe the guards at your gates won't know anything about it. Also, they are afraid of the valley, so even if they know you're there, they won't dare enter. It might be the best choice for now, for you."

Zora nodded. "True. But what about you?"

"I should go back and talk to my brother."

"He wants you killed! I didn't face a freaking lion and got an arrow on my shoulder and cuts on my arms for you to waste your life. Come to the Dark Valley. You'll be safe there. I mean, safe from your brother, at least. There are the shadow creatures, but we're good at fighting them."

"I know you're good."

"Lie down and rest, then, and I'll—"

He was getting out of the cart. "No. I'll conduct. You're hurt, remember?"

"Are you sure?"

"Yes, I'm feeling better."

They both sat in the front. Zora had no clue what would

happen back home, if someone would catch them on the way, and her shoulder hurt a lot. The worst part was realizing how much she'd enjoyed kissing Griffin, even knowing well about him and Alegra, knowing well he was in love with the princess, knowing well he'd never love Zora back. Her heart—and mouth, and hands—were so dumb. She'd need to keep her wits and fight them.

RIADNE RETREATED TO HER ROOM, exhausted. What had she done? Used more magic than she could. For what? It made no sense. At least Kiran changed from wanting her dead to looking at her in adoration. The people in the arena left confused as to what they had seen, other than the girl killing the lion.

Why had she done it? A year planning revenge. It had been so close. Three brothers in love with her, tearing each other apart. Griffin had almost literally been torn apart. The perfect revenge for everything that family had done to her people. And yet she had been weak when it was time to be strong.

She had never gotten close to either Kiran or Larzen. But with Griffin, there was this youthful innocence, this intensity. She'd told herself it had been for fun. And yet, it might have made her weak.

And the stupid Dark Valley girl? Riadne had let her go. After trying to scare her, send her away, perhaps even kill her. She'd known it. From the moment she'd seen him gawking at her in that library, she'd known the girl would be a problem. And still, in the arena, Riadne pitied the girl in her desperation and courage. Compassion, what a stupid feeling.

Everything was so confusing. She wished she could speak

to her brother, but knew that he was busy, too, keeping the real Alegra, making sure the Linaria kingdom didn't notice anything. Sometimes Riadne wasn't even sure what was right and what was wrong. Sometimes she even wondered if she really wanted to go through with her revenge. But it wasn't about her, but about her people. It was her duty. And now she would need to find another way for the brothers to tear each other apart.

GRIFFIN HAD ALWAYS WANTED to visit the Dark Valley and finally was going to do it. Under such unexpected circumstances. He glanced at Zora, sitting beside him. Even in his confusion, he'd seen her, he'd heard her plea, her horrifying "please" that had haunted him. And it made sense, now. He'd seen it after asking the basin if Alegra loved him. But he'd been under the impression the princess had cared for him. And it had been Zora.

A few more things were clear, as he remembered seeing the Dark Valley girl walking towards him with the rising sun, when he thought she was a goddess. He remembered the way she looked at that library in awe, her eyes so filled with wonder, then again with that expression looking at the artists in the opening of the games. Griffin had been terrified of something bad happening to her, of her getting hurt. Only now the reason came to him.

He then remembered the night she had cared for him. Sweet, soft, calming hands, and a nightmare-free night. The confusion had been Alegra, as if she had made him forget, as if... Perhaps the princess had done something. Or maybe he was making excuses. He couldn't blame Zora for wanting nothing with him. And she was right. He had to clear his mind first. Understand his feelings. Then get rid of that stupid curse. To make matters worse, he had missed the opportunity to get the one tool that could help him.

He turned to Zora. "You won."

"What?"

"The Blood Cup. It's yours."

She rolled her eyes. "Oh, right. I guess I'll go back and ask your brother to give it to me. I'm sure he'll be delighted."

Griffin shook his head. "It's not as simple."

She snorted. "Simple?"

"You have to find it."

Zora frowned. "Let me get this straight. So you hosted a competition to give a prize that you don't know where it is?"

"The winner can find it. And can take it. Did you kill the lion?"

"Yes."

She didn't sound happy. No wonder.

Perhaps she'd never get the cup. Even if she got it, what good would it do to Griffin? Perhaps he was doomed, and this had been a losing game from the start. That curse. One good reason to stay away from Zora.

The curse. He stopped. "Tonight we'll have a new moon."

"Is it a problem?"

Griffin sighed. For the first time in his life, he was away from his safe room, away from any place that could contain him, and to make matters worse, Zora would find out what he was. There wasn't much time before the sun set and he needed a solution, quickly.

"What is it?" she insisted.

"It's..." He closed his eyes. "There will be a monster tonight."

She pointed to the pommel of her sword on her back. "I can deal with monsters." She had that same bravado that once he'd thought was exaggerated. Now, he wasn't so sure.

He had to tell her the truth. There was no time to go around it, no time to come up with a story. He gathered the strength to say the hardest words he'd ever said in his life. "The monster's me."

COMING SOON

The Curse and the Prince

Don't boo me for the ending. The story in *The Cup and the Prince* finished, right?

But yes, there's more coming, and we'll follow Zora and the prince as they face brand new challenges.

The series *Kingdom of Curses and Shadows* continues in *The Curse and the Prince*. Find it here:

dayleitao.com/books/curse-prince/

ABOUT THE AUTHOR

I love to give life to characters and connect with readers. I'm originally from Brazil and I live in Montreal, Canada.

You can check my ramblings at my blog and also sign up for my newsletter and get an exclusive short story which is a prequel to *The Cup and the Prince at:*

dayleitao.com